The Other
Face

LORRAINE WAIT

For my
precious niece
Bonnie

With love from
Lorraine

A.

DEDICATION

For my dear husband, Wayne, for his unfailing patience and helpful advice.

CHAPTER 1

Sharon Roberts leaned back in her beige leather recliner and closed her eyes, her pen-holding hand resting on her lap pillow desk. She had purposely arranged her evening for quiet relaxation to prepare herself for the challenge she would be facing the next morning. While her dinner had been cooking in the microwave, she had pulled off her tight jeans and cuddled up in her comfy velveteen hooded top and pants. To make certain she could relax for the whole evening, she had piled on the TV table beside her chair, the newspaper, her thermos of ice-water, crossword puzzle books and several squares of dark chocolate. She liked to call them her "happiness" supplies. They amused her after dinner, especially when the TV commercials were playing. Tonight was no different, her stomach was full and her body relaxed, but her mind was elsewhere.

****

Meanwhile, in a care facility on the other side of town, someone else was also sitting, but with a body alert and listening, and a mind focused like a laser on the goal, to bring death to an innocent frail soul.

****

A cool September evening breeze stirred the vertical blinds of the sliding patio door on Sharon's left. The remains of her now cold dinner sat on the TV table, the television's evening news floated off, unnoticed, into the room around her, while she tried to imagine tomorrow's big day, back at her old Vancouver law office. She had been jotting down a few names on her notepad, and between sipping water, staring unfocussed at the ceiling, knuckling her forehead, rubbing her eyes and occasionally stabbing at the morsels on her dinner plate, she had hoped to feel more prepared for the day ahead by making notes. It was a practice she had developed at law school, where she had been determined to stay near the top of her classes.

She was nervous about returning to work full time as a legal assistant after three years of attending university, working only temporary office assignments between study terms. After her husband had died four years ago, feeling that she should do something special with her life to add some worth to his death, she had decided to become a lawyer, hoping that his life insurance monies could put her through law school.

Insurance had paid off the mortgage on their apartment, and Sharon had put herself on a strict budget, but she knew she would run out of money before the next term ended.

The decision to interrupt her studies had been difficult for Sharon, wavering between taking out a mortgage loan, asking her Aunt Desi for financial help, or returning to work. After the phone call last month from Doug Burns, the personnel manager of her old office, she had started another list of the three options she felt were available, listing the pros and cons. She knew that sitting in front of her bank manager to arrange a new mortgage loan would make her stomach churn - that awful queezy feeling whenever her fate was in the hands of someone else. On the other hand, she would feel even worse in asking her Aunt for help although her request would be granted in a heartbeat, freely and unconditionally. She didn't want to do anything that would change the loving closeness they had between them.

Feeling that somehow the fates were making her decision for her, she had accepted Burns' assignment. It seemed like the easy way out, with no emotional turmoil and no strings attached. She had rationalized that a temporary break away from the academic corridors back to the real world, and the resulting financial benefits, might even be good for her. The conditions that Burns offered had surprised and intrigued her. She would return to assist one of the partners in the firm and would receive an unusually generous benefit package which included the flexibility Sharon needed to continue with at least part-time studies.

The events of the last year had taken their emotional toll. Her uncle Donald, who had virtually adopted Sharon in her 21st year after her parents had died in a boating accident, had himself died in early January, leaving his widow Desiree heartbroken.

Every weekend for four months after his death Sharon had traveled to their cosy waterfront cottage on Vancouver Island to be with Desi and help her get Donald's estate in order. She had felt thankful that her legal experience had prepared her for dealing with wills and estates, as it had when her husband had succumbed to lung cancer four years previously. Desi, as tiny and frail as she was, had tried to keep on a brave face and deal with all the paperwork, but sobbed with relief and happiness whenever Sharon arrived.

It had been nearly a year ago that Sharon had started longing for a break from all the studying and writing. She had been surprised at the sense of boredom that had been creeping into her afternoons, as she had struggled to stay awake during the dry lectures.

She had even started to doubt whether becoming a lawyer would actually help her feel that her husband hadn't died in vain. She hoped that Doug Burns' offer, and the resulting change in pace for her, might bring back some enthusiasm for finishing her law degree.

Tomorrow wasn't going to be easy for her, to step back through the doors of Stewart, Hird & Company after three years. Being an almost obsessive list-maker since high school, when she used the activity to calm herself before exams, she had wanted to remind herself of the names of the other legal assistants and staff at the office. Although she knew it wasn't necessary, she felt remembering their names was the least she could do in return for all the gentle concern they had shown during her late husband's illness and subsequent death.

Doug Burns' name had been at the top of her list. She knew his office would be her first destination when she reached the office, to sign employment and tax forms and get a briefing on her assignment.

She smiled as she imagined the office and the long hallway to Doug Burns' office at the other end of the 19th floor, remembering the smell of freshly brewed coffee from behind the lunchroom door that she would pass on the way to his office.

She could see the three south-facing work stations, each containing at least four secretarial desks, she would pass on her way down the hallway. Between the work stations, she would pass several closed, wood-paneled doors with their gold name-plates for each lawyer.

Four years ago, Sharon's own work station had been the first one after the reception area, and from her chair Sharon had been able to see the whole length of the carpeted hallway, and the movement of people in and out of the doors along it. The doors were always shut, and Sharon recalled the game she had often played as she had walked past each door, guessing what could be going on behind it.

Working on her list, she was surprised at how easily her memory popped out the names of the staff and the lawyers, and at the anticipation she was feeling about working with them again. That was her biggest discovery, she thought, "Here I am, Mrs. Shyness herself, actually looking forward to working with people again! Maybe going back to University was actually good for me."

Her reverie was interrupted with the jarring ring of the phone beside her, and all her good intentions of preparation flew out the window as she recognized the soft lilt of her aunt's French accent.

" Hello my dear, 'ow are you?"

"Ah, Aunt Desiree, I'm so glad you phoned."

"I hope it is okay to call; it is getting dark, but I wanted to hear your voice."

"Of course, you know you can phone me any time."

"I'm feeling sleepy today, I think my bones know my birthday is coming in a few weeks."

"I'm so sorry, Desi. I had planned to call you this evening, but I must have fallen asleep in my chair. I guess we're both sleepyheads today. Are you feeling okay?"

"Well, I am maybe a little sad, because Donald's prize chrysanthemums have bloomed and they are so beautiful, and he is not here to enjoy them."

"My poor sweetie, I wish I could be there to give you a big hug."

"Oh, oui. I would love for you to come and have a holiday here with me."

"I'm so sorry, sweetheart, I'm stuck here on the Mainland for the next little while. I've agreed to go back to work at my old law office, and I start there tomorrow."

"But I thought you were going to school."

"I've finished my semester, and decided to take a break. I'll probably sign up again after next summer, or if I can manage maybe even for next Spring."

"That's good. I am so proud of you. You will be a good lawyer."

"Thank you, my sweetie. I just hope I can make it. It's a lot of hard work."

"I wish I could help you somehow."

"Just being able to get away to the Island to visit with you is a big help."

"Maybe I could come to stay with you for a while, would that be okay? I can make some of my special dinners and pastries for you and help with shopping."

"Ooh, that sounds wonderful! We can do something special for your birthday and we'll have fun going to movies and the malls."

"It will make me very happy to visit you."

"Me too. You could spend the whole winter here with me."

"Are you sure?" and then, "When would you like me to come?"

"I can spend next weekend on the Island and bring you back with me on Sunday. "

"Are you sure you won't mind? I don't want to be any trouble."

"Now you stop that, my little Silly Billy, I love it when we can be together, and you know I enjoy the ferry rides. I can get over there late Friday after work, and then drive up to your place early Saturday morning. We could use all day Saturday to pack your belongings and close up your cottage and then go out for a nice seafood dinner at our favorite place, what do you think?"

"You are so precious, my darling. I am so glad to have you, and you have been such a help to me since Donald died..."

Sharon could feel the sadness creeping into Desi's voice, "Well, I love you to bits. Just think about how much fun we'll have when you get here."

Desi twittered, "Oh yes, our cribbage and scrabble games, that will keep my thoughts busy. And I can visit the library on your street and help keep your apartment tidy."

"Now, Desi, I'm not bringing you back to be my housekeeper. Just having you here to greet me after work will brighten my days."

"I can hardly wait, and I think I will maybe see your lawyers about my Will too, it might need changing now that Donald is gone..."

"I think I remember looking at your will last winter. It's probably fine, but I know that it's always a good idea to have a will checked every few years anyway. Mr. Fisher would enjoy meeting you..."

"Is that who you will be working for?"

"No, but I worked for him a few years ago - I think you'll like him. He has a way with the ladies."

Desi giggled, "Oh my! Such excitement for me. I won't be able to sleep tonight."

"Me neither, starting all over again...."

"Oh, I am so sorry my dear, I must let you get to bed so that you can be ready for your new job tomorrow."

"That's okay Desi, we'll talk again when I get to the Island on Friday."

After their goodbyes, Sharon knew she wouldn't accomplish anything else that evening, and gathered up her dishes and supplies and dumped them onto the kitchen counter, thinking "I'll clean all that up tomorrow after work," her mind already preparing for her aunt's visit.

While Sharon curled up under her blankets, thinking about her aunt, another elderly woman on the other side of the city was about to become the victim of someone whose grim determination would threaten several other lives, including Sharon's.

CHAPTER 2

In a convalescent home on the west side of the City, many miles from Sharon's east-side apartment, and not aware that a crime had taken place, the nurse stood at her medicine cart in the hallway beside the slightly ajar door. She was preparing the medicines, as prescribed in the open loose leaf binder perched on top of the cart, marking her progress on the patient's chart, and subconsciously listening for the expected peaceful purring snore from the room.

The steady background hum of the ceiling fans and the slowly-beeping monitor in the next patient's room muffled her soft footsteps, as she picked up the small paper cup of pills and her flashlight and carefully pushed open the door to walk to the bedside of the white-haired frail form.

"Mary, my dear, it's me, Brenda. It's time for your evening pills..."

As she shone the flashlight onto the pillow beside Mary, suddenly noticing the unusual silence, she gasped, then quickly felt for a pulse at her favorite patient's cold wrist. "Oh no, no. Mary. Mary! Please wake up!"

She pulled the oxygen mask into place over Mary's slack mouth, trying to stir Mary to take a breath, as she switched on the controls. Knowing that a "Do not Resuscitate" order had been signed several days before, she left the oxygen mask in place and ran out to the nursing station, calling "Trudy, help! I think we're losing Mary!"

Trudy, the senior nurse on duty that night, looked up from behind her desk, put down her glasses, and stood to her full 6-foot height, taking a long slow breath before following Brenda calmly and slowly into the room, where she immediately turned on the main lights. The blue-white fingertips and gray pallor told their own story, confirmed by the cool temperature of the body.

Trudy removed the oxygen mask and pulled the curtains closed around the bed.

"None of that crying now, Brenda, we've got things to do. Get her charts and phone for our resident."

"She was so sweet, and seemed to be doing so well, I don't understand..She was talking just yesterday about calling her lawyer to make another change in her Will."

Brenda knew she was babbling. It was her nervous reaction to death. "I think we are supposed to call her lawyers, that big law firm downtown, Stewart something or other. That's the only contact number we have in her file, I don't think she had any family."

"Brenda, settle down. We'll go through her file and make calls in the morning. The lawyer won't be available at this time of night anyway."

"I don't know how you stay so calm, Trudy. I'm just so shaken right now, losing such a dear person. She was one of my favorite patients. It's just so sad, she slipped away without letting us know, and we had lots of good talks over the last few months. I'll miss her so much," sniffled Brenda as she sat down at the nursing station, wiping her eyes, to work through the pages in her patient's binder.

Neither of them had noticed the rumpled-looking, baseball-capped person who had been sitting just inside the small family lounge at the far end of the hallway.

Neither had they seen nor heard the quiet opening of and quick departure through the exit door, or the grim smile of satisfaction which appeared on the face of the person whose evil deed had apparently produced the desired result.

CHAPTER 3

The next morning, waking before her alarm sounded, Sharon enjoyed a long, trembling stretch. Although she felt like rolling over and curling up under the blankets, she knew a leisurely shower and a coffee-fueled scan through the newspaper would be a more comfortable start to the day ahead.

Ninety minutes later, happy she was able to find an empty seat next to the window on the transit train, she nestled down into her turned-up collar and rested her head against the glass, closing her eyes behind her sunglasses. Now that she wasn't using her commuting time for studying, she relaxed into her favorite habit of daydreaming on the train, hoping she wouldn't fall asleep and miss the mechanical voice announcing her destination station.

Lulled into a dreamy state by the hum and gentle rocking of the train, occasionally distracted by the screech of the train's wheels on the curves, Sharon replayed the phone conversation with her elderly aunt Desi. It reminded her of the summer, after her 17th birthday, when she had first become close to her uncle and aunt during her stay with them in their southern California home. Her Uncle Donald had phoned and asked to speak directly with Sharon. He asked Sharon if she would like to spend the summer months with them.

"I'd love to come. What an adventure!" Sharon gushed over the phone to her Uncle Donald. "But I'll need to talk to Mom and Dad to see if its okay."

"I've already talked to your Mother. I used my influence as her much older brother," Donald chuckled, "and she has agreed you are a big girl now, and she and your father will allow you to come to sunny California."

"I could take the Greyhound bus, then it won't cost very much."

"Well, that will certainly be an adventure. It will be non-stop until you reach Los Angeles, you know."

Although she had seen them several times during her childhood when they had visited Vancouver, it wasn't until that summer that she had sensed her uncle's deep affection for her and her mother, and his wish to be closer to family. She could almost see him now, the bemused pleasure showing in his eyes, as he had watched the fun and laughter that bounced between his niece Sharon and his beloved Desi.

"Well, my darling Donald, while you are working today, Sharon and I will be going shopping." Desi announced as she pulled her gold curls up into a ponytail. "She is now my daughter. You must tell your sister that I have adopted Sharon and she must agree that we will share her.

"I'm sure she won't mind," Donald smiled a gentle look at Desi, "She knows that we have no other family."

"We have the best family in the world." Desi sidled up to Sharon, hugging her, "We will shop until we drop." Desi winked up at Sharon, a mischievous smile on her face.

"You girls behave yourselves," laughed Donald. "I don't want to send out a truck to get you. If you are both good, I'll take you out for dinner tonight."

"You see, Sharon, isn't he just the sweetest soul ever?" smiled Desi. "He knows we will be tired after shopping all day, and doesn't want us to be slaving over the stove again."

Sharon smiled at both of them as she hugged Desi closer to her, "You two are like honeymooners, I just love you both to bits."

Seven years after Sharon's visit to their California home, Donald had retired and they had purchased their waterfront cottage on the east coast of Vancouver Island. Sharon had been delighted to have them so close. She and her husband had always preferred the Island for holidays, and those relaxing ferry rides they loved would now also bring the additional pleasure of family visits with her uncle and aunt, sitting on their full-length front porch, looking over the ocean in front of them.

Sharon's reverie of the island hideaway was suddenly interrupted by the mechanical voice announcing her transit station. Giving her head a slight shake to focus on her surroundings, she stood up quickly and grabbed a stanchion to steady herself while the train came to a stop at the platform.

The main lobby of the 20-storey office building was slowly awakening, as the retail shops on the ground floor rolled up their clattering metal security gates, like a sleeping mechanical monster opening one eye after another, to watch its next victim enter the hall and walk by.

Outside on this September morning, the sky was a blinding light blue, and the air was cool and damp, almost cold in the wind. Pushed by the wind through the doors, with hands up to adjust windblown hair or hats, the office workers hurried down the long tiled hallway to the elevators.

Walking along the hallway to the main lobby, Sharon slowed to check her reflection in the polished shop windows, her leather-gloved hand reaching to remove her sunglasses and brush wisps of her dark auburn hair from her cheeks. Turning toward the elevators, she quickened her pace, her high heels clicking on the polished floors.

She felt the glances of several of the people standing at the elevators, and although there were several "good mornings" among the group crowding with her into the express elevator, no one spoke directly to her.

Bracing for the ride with a few yawns, a throat clearing, a shuffle of feet, the occupants turned to face the closing elevator doors and stare up at the floor numbers lighting up, one by one. Their metal box jumped into its upward rush to the 15th floor before its first stop to spit out a few of its occupants. The sleepy elevator music did nothing to settle Sharon's reaction to the sudden momentum each time the doors closed in front of her.

Stepping off the elevator at the 19th floor, Sharon's stomach fluttered slightly as she looked through the wide opening into the reception room. She smiled as she recognized a familiar incongruous sound from the richly carpeted softly-lit room, "Teri's gold bracelets" she thought. "At least I'll know somebody here besides Mr. Burns."

She turned left from the elevator, toward the women's lounge and washroom, and once inside, hung up her coat. Checking her reflection in the full-length mirror that covered one wall, she brushed her hands down the sides of her slim skirt to smooth and straighten it. Although heels were not her favorite shoe, she liked the way they enhanced her long slim legs.

The only other occupant in the washroom was a sour-faced woman in her fifties, sitting in one of the soft leather armchairs, filing her nails. "I don't recognize her," Sharon thought, hesitating to greet her, "Doesn't look like a 'good morning' type."

The woman didn't look up to acknowledge Sharon's presence or her movement toward the door as she picked up her bag to re-enter the lobby. "It feels like forever since I've worked here, I guess there'll be lots of people I don't know."

Sharon pushed open the door and before she could take a step, was enveloped with an enthusiastic hug from the voluptuous woman who had been reaching for the door handle. A wide, bright-red smile and an excited, "Well, look who's here!" greeted her. "Sharon Roberts, I'll be darned. I thought you'd be remarried and having babies by now! Look at you - you look wonderful!"

Sharon returned the hug with a smile, noticing that her former workmate still wore her long, dark false eyelashes, "Hi Anna, good to see your beautiful Italian smile." She hesitated. "No, I'm not married, just working my way through law school. Life insurance only goes so far, you know."

"Good for you! I'm so happy to see you back. You must have been called in for Mr. Westbrook, the old goat."

Sharon laughed and felt the flutter in her stomach start again. "Is he that bad?"

"Well, he wants shorthand secretaries for one thing, so he can pace back and forth and wave his arms while he's dictating."

"That's okay, I like using my shorthand..."

"That's not all. He arranged for his assistant's work station to be in a separate cubicle. It's a lonely job. He's got this 'thing' about idle office chitchat."

"Guess I'll have my work cut out for me today" replied Sharon as she stepped away from the door. "Well, Anna, we'll see you at coffee."

By now the second elevator had spilled out its assortment of secretaries and lawyers, each group breaking into separate directions, the doorway to the ladies lounge being held open by the steady stream of women, removing their gloves, coats and jackets on their way in.

Sharon turned to enter the reception area. It had been over three years since she had worked at the law firm of Stewart, Hird & Company, one of the largest and most successful firms in the Vancouver metropolitan area. By comparison, the stimulating but relatively relaxing months she had spent at the University seemed like a dream as she took a big breath to adjust to the pressurized working atmosphere.

As she stepped from the noisy tiles of the lobby onto the plush carpeting, she heard a familiar voice from behind the reception counter to her right, "Well, hello my long-lost commuting buddy. I see that Mr. Burns finally got hold of the elusive Mrs. Roberts!"

Sharon walked past and behind the reception counter, and bent down to hug the speaker, whose brightly painted, long nails were busy pushing buttons on the phone switchboard, her armful of bracelets jangling. After waiting for a lull in the frantic activity in front of her, Sharon whispered "Hi, Teri, good to see you. How's everything going?"

"Great, as usual. Still pushing people's buttons, as you can see!", she laughed, "We haven't heard from you for so long. Where have you been for the last couple of years?"

Sharon hesitated as several more calls interrupted Teri's attention, watching with amusement as Teri flew through the motions of connecting conversations.

Teri Telford, with her up-swept blond hair and long dangling earrings, was just tall enough, by stretching up in her chair, to see over the counter of her receptionist station. She had been the switchboard operator and receptionist for the law firm for over twenty years, and had turned down every offer for promotion within the office. Sharon knew that Teri preferred the variety and excitement of working at the front desk.

Teri, too, had been widowed at a relatively young age, but had remarried soon afterward, often joking about her "Old George" and how he had rescued her from poverty and widowhood and how he loved his annual habit of giving her another gold bangle on their anniversary.

Sharon had enjoyed Teri's understanding ear on their evening rides home, helping her cope during the months her husband was dying from lung cancer. Teri's down-to-earth common sense, coupled with a wicked sense of humor, often transformed Sharon's most downcast moments into mutual giggling fits.

Teri was the cheerful traffic "walk signal" in the sombre atmosphere of the waiting room, with its over-stuffed leather chairs. Her cutting wit and playfulness had kept many of the lawyers at bay, but she had also gained a reputation for putting clients, usually nervous or impatient, at complete ease with her flashing smile and light-hearted chatter. She seemed to enjoy entertaining visitors while they waited for their lawyer or the legal assistants to escort them back to the inner reaches of the office.

Teri was also the most direct and reliable source for office grapevine news. Sharon had enjoying watching Teri's fun-loving and outrageous flirting, and her compete reversal of expression if rudeness, dishonesty or patronization touched her.

At a slight break in the frantic phone activity, Sharon answered, "Oh, I've just been hanging around. University courses, etcetera, and last summer I worked for a firm in Burnaby. Several visits to the Island, a cruise with my aunt to Mexico in April, just trying to keep a good balance, you know." She paused. "Good heavens those phones are busy"

"Lucky duck, you, what a life. Yup, it's the Monday morning crazies who've been waiting all weekend to dial our number," chuckled Teri as another call light lit her board.

"Well, I'd better report to Mr. Burns right away. Don't want trouble on my first day."

"See you at coffee" winked Teri as she turned back to the demanding blinking lights on her call center.

As she hurried down the long carpeted hall to the manager's office, Sharon touched her hair and brushed imaginary lint from her shoulders. She knew that it would not be a relaxing day. She had heard enough about Michael Westbrook to be prepared for the worst.

He had joined the firm the year before Sharon had left it, and although she had never had to work directly for him during that time, she had been slightly curious about him, having heard stories of his steely-eyed awareness and memory. He was tall and good-looking, much older than Sharon, and seemed to have a following of admiring lawyers in the law firm.

Sharon had seen several newspaper reports of the trials that Westbrook had won for his clients, which included several large corporations. The articles described his Courtroom manner as quiet and low-key. She had noticed that photos of him almost always portrayed a serious direct gaze under his dark frowning brows, and she had marveled at the awe-stricken tone of reports of "a ruthless genius hidden behind a gentle smile", and "His tactics have left yet another opponent scrambling", and "He turned the opposing team into laughing stock."

And now she had agreed to walk into that den and hand-feed the lion!

Approaching the open door of the office manager, Douglas Burns, Sharon could see him laughing into the telephone propped between his ear and shoulder, his chair balancing precariously on its rear feet.

Seeing Sharon at the door, he stopped flipping the end of his tie against his ample, white-shirted stomach and motioned for her to sit down in the chair in front of his desk. He sat forward, his chair stopped in its balancing act with a light thud, and he fumbled to button the front of his conservative gray jacket. He ran his fingers along the right side of his head and stood up to button his jacket as he ended the phone conversation.

"Sure Ben, I'll see what I can do. Talk to you later." As he returned the phone to its cradle, he grinned happily. "Well now, my dear Sharon, am I glad to see you. C'mon, I'll show you where you'll be sitting." He came around to the front of his desk, shook her hand, and gently guided her with his hand at her elbow, to the passageway leading away to the right of his office. "You're looking healthy and tanned."

"Thank you. How have you been?"

"Fine, just fine. I'll be even better after next week. I'm going on holidays."

"Anywhere exciting?"

"No, just up to the lake. You haven't worked for Michael before, have you? " he asked as he guided Sharon to an alcove on her right, just beyond a closed door bearing a brass and black nameplate "Michael Westbrook".

"No, is that good or bad?" asked Sharon, almost absent-mindedly, as she admired the view from her work station of the Vancouver harbor and the mountains behind it. The large Canada flag on the waterfront building below her was blowing straight out to the left, reminding Sharon of the cold wintry East wind that had blown her into the building that morning.

"You'll be fine with your brains and shorthand. He's one of our die-hards who hates to dictate to a machine, and his full-time secretary is currently on long-term sick leave. None of the other secretaries were willing to abandon their own lawyers for a chance to work with Michael, even with a big increase in wages." He paused as he grinned at Sharon, "And the last secretary we hired from a temp agency just got up and walked out after two days.

"Ooh, that sounds bad," laughed Sharon, as she sat down in the chair at the desk and looked up at Burns. Using her foot to push her purse under the bottom drawer of the desk, she asked "I gather the die-hard 'lives' in this office beside me?"

"You've got it."

"Okay, and everything else is pretty much the same?"

"Yes. Lulu still runs me and the accounting department, there's a few new girls in the filing room, and we've added another photocopy room at the other end of the office. Dennis Fisher has a new secretary, she sits over there. Burns motioned to one of the four desks in the alcove across the hallway from Sharon's.

"She should be in soon. Her name is Betty Campbell."

They had passed only three other secretaries on their way to Sharon's desk, as it was not yet 9:00 AM. Sharon remembered that most of the secretaries seemed to spend the last few minutes in the ladies room primping and chatting, or in the coffee room enjoying their last cigarette and coffee before fanning throughout the office to their desks.

"When does Mr. Westbrook usually come in?"

"I think it's usually around eight, but today he's not supposed to be in until around 9:30 or 10:00." He turned back toward his own office with "I'll bring you some forms to fill in later. Come and see me if you need help settling in."

Sharon answered, "Thanks, Doug, will do." She turned back toward her work station, opening the drawers and cupboards to check for supplies. She pulled the garbage can from beneath the counter and started filling it with twisted, useless paper clips and balls of crumpled paper she found in the drawers. She found a small pad of note paper and started making a list of supplies she would need, thinking "Good God, how could anyone work in this mess?"

She emptied the top drawer of its salvageable supplies, then pulled the whole drawer out and rested the corner of it in the waste basket as she knocked the dust, eraser shavings, bent paper clips and bits of paper out. She worked quickly and as quietly as possible, using a tissue from her jacket pocket to wipe away dust from the counter and around the keyboard and computer.

A few minutes later, as she walked back from the filing room with an armful of supplies, she quickened her pace as she heard the murmur of female voices chase her from down the hallway. "It must be 9:00 o'clock" she thought, as a male voice called, "Well, look who's back, running as usual!"

Sharon continued her quick pace and turned to smile, "Oh, Hi Mr. Fisher, how are you?" She was glad that this assignment wasn't acting as Dennis Fisher's assistant, although she was now wondering if working for Michael Westbrook would be even less appealing.

"Fine, just fine. Have you met my new secretary yet?"

"No, not yet. She sits there, doesn't she?", motioning with her head.

Sharon leaned to put her burden on her desk, and immediately sat down, well aware that Fisher was right behind her, eyeing her legs. She had learned early in her years of working at Stewart & Company to keep him at a distance and to position herself so that his mischievous grinning gaze had restricted freedom of travel over parts of her anatomy.

The last time she had worked for him had been an uncomfortably warm but thankfully temporary assignment. Although it had been summertime, she had adjusted her wardrobe during those two weeks, wearing her highest-necked, long-sleeved tops, covered with loose jackets, vests or sweaters, only to discover that his imagination seemed to compensate for what he couldn't see.

His straight blond hair often hung in his eyes, and Sharon was sure that the angle at which he tipped his head was as much to keep the hair out of his eyes as it was to sneak sidelong glances at the female anatomies in his vicinity. He had once teased Sharon with "I've heard that women with very long hair pinned up in a bun are secret sexpots." Soon after that remark, Sharon had surprised her favorite hairdresser, with her request for a new, very short hairstyle.

Over the years, as Sharon had developed a reputation in the firm as a no-nonsense hard worker, she had been able to stare Fisher down, laughingly calling him a lecherous old man enough times that he treated her, as he had learned to treat the senior female lawyer in the firm, with begrudging respect.

Sharon remembered that Dennis Fisher was often the subject of giggling gossip in the office, as the secretaries compared notes on his most recent stumble into the quick-sand of body watching.

He had developed the habit of each morning telling at least one funny story or joke to the secretaries next to his office. More than once he was the victim of a mischievous arrangement among his audience to "accidentally" expose some part of their anatomy to see if he could finish his sentence or remember the punchline of his story.

"Oh, here comes Betty now," said Fisher, as he backed into Sharon's alcove to let his secretary get to her desk. "Betty, have you met Sharon?"

"No, pleased to meet you," said the sour face that Sharon had seen earlier that morning.

"Hello, Betty," said Sharon as the woman turned her back and sat at her desk.

Fisher leaned over Sharon's desk and whispered, "She's mean, watch out," then grinned his way back to his office.

Dennis Fisher had developed such a reputation among the secretaries that they had avoided being alone with him whenever possible, a fact known to Doug Burns, who had always managed to hire a no-nonsense woman who could keep Fisher under control.

Among the partners in the law firm, however, as well as an ever-widening stream of "little old ladies", Fisher was known for his expertise in handling wills and estates. He spent a good deal of his time on the phone, admiring his shiny shoes as he propped his short legs up on the windowsill, or inspecting the cut of his fingernails while advising this lawyer or that soon-to-be wealthy widow on the finer points of his law specialty. Clients were often heard to remark, "He's such a nice man, so kind," as they were escorted from Fisher's office by his assistant. His long-suffering assistant, lying through her teeth, would agree.

Two other legal assistants arrived at the 4-person work station across from Sharon, blithely chirping "Good Morning" to the non-responsive Betty. Anna Mosconi waved at Sharon and sat down at her work station, facing Sharon from across the hallway. A tall, model-like blond, Julia Ashley, was settling into her desk beside Anna's, when Anna's lifted eyebrows and sudden motioning of her head warned Sharon that Michael Westbrook was coming up behind her. She hurriedly put the rest of her supplies away, thinking "Oh darn, he's early".

She heard his door opening, and then his firm flat voice, as he stepped into his office, asking "Bring your book in, please."

With raised eyebrows and a slight shrug of her shoulder, Sharon gathered up her notebook and several pencils, then winked at Anna to acknowledge her thumbs-up and "Good Luck" gestures.

"Thanks, I might need it," Sharon nodded, and stepped lightly through the doorway toward the chairs in front of Westbrook's desk.

As Sharon leaned to pull one of the chairs slightly away from Westbrook's desk, she heard a soft "Shut the door" spoken to the letter he was holding in front of his face.

"Okay, Mr. Rude" thought Sharon, "I'll play your little game," as she closed the door then sat in the chair closest to the window with the same view of the Vancouver harbor as her own. She sat waiting for his first words, her pencil poised and ready to scribble her Pitman shorthand onto the notepad on her knee.

Sharon filled the long quiet pause that followed by doodling in the corners of her notebook and outlining the holes along the top of the coil-bound book with scallops, then retracing the designs until they were dark and thick. His sudden throat-clearing cough startled her into looking up at him.

With an almost pained look on his face, he said "Now, I want you to get something straight before we even start" as he pressed the tips of his fingers together and used his thumbs to rub his chest, "I don't want you to make any decisions or advise any of my clients unless you have checked with me first, or you are sure that you know what you are doing. If you have any questions about any of my dictation, ask me about it first, don't go changing anything on your own."

"I understand," Sharon said in the most self-assured voice she could muster, wondering to herself what terrible mistakes his other secretaries had made to make him come down so heavily on her without provocation. She could feel her jaw tightening up, ready for the next orders, when he asked,

"What's your name?"

Surprised by the sudden change in tactics, she smiled "Sharon Roberts", looking directly into his dark blue eyes, where she noticed, thankfully, that a smile passed momentarily across his face before he abruptly sat forward in his chair and picked up a pen.

"Roberts, hmmm..." as he wrote something in the open loose leaf book lying next to his right hand. "The widow Roberts?

"Yes, for about four years now," answered Sharon, surprised that he knew anything about her.

Abruptly he closed the book, picked up a folder laying at the side of his desk and dropped it onto his desk blotter. He opened the folder and lifted a few pages before picking up a pen and speaking down toward the file, "Okay, first of all, on the Hydro vs. Smith file, do a letter to Clyde & Company on Hastings..."

Sharon hurriedly scribbled notes, ready for further dictation, when a loud knock at the door was followed by the abrupt entry of Mr. Hird, the fourth most senior partner in the law firm of thirty-five men. He was a tall, gaunt man in his early seventies, only a few years older than Westbrook.

While adjusting his small metal-framed glasses on his large beaked nose, Hird announced "Just got a call from the hospital - our rich old widow Mary Boyle died last night. Get your articling students to order the death certificate and start the Probate process," and, as he dropped the file onto the side of Michael's desk, "I want to get that Executor fee coming in as soon as possible." He immediately turned back through the door and closed it, with no indication he expected a response. Sharon felt invisible.

"Yes, Sir. Right away, Sir!" Westbrook muttered, his voice dripping with sarcasm as he dropped the file to the floor on his right.

Sharon looked up at him, surprised by his tone, and then quickly glanced at the door to see if it was closed when she saw Westbrook mouth the word "Bastard!"

Westbrook noticed her wide-eyed surprise and said "Sorry," as he picked up his pen. "Okay, where was I?"

For the next hour, with the coil notebook propped on her crossed knee, Sharon filled page after page with shorthand notes and arrows and asterisks as she made certain that what she was hearing could be transcribed correctly. Letters, Writs, Affidavits and file memos that were apparently in Westbrook's full view on the ceiling and walls of his office came tumbling from his mouth. Michael dictated at a relentless speed, most of the time leaning precariously back in his black leather executive chair, sitting up only briefly as he looked at each file or handed files and papers to Sharon after he had finished with each item.

The pile of documents and files on the chair beside Sharon grew steadily, and the last few items were in danger of sliding off, when Sharon's stomach growled it's readiness for the morning coffee break. Between steadying the tipping pile of documents, and trying to swallow down her hunger pangs, Sharon started to wonder if the marathon dictating session would ever end, when Michael slowed his pace.

She felt that somehow she had passed his first test, as she had managed to keep up with him the whole time, without asking him to repeat anything or slow down. Although she had some questions about some of his instructions, she was determined to figure them out on her own by reviewing the files in the safety and privacy of her own desk.

"Okay, you can go for coffee now; I think your stomach is trying to tell me something."

Sharon giggled slightly, then blushed a sheepish "Thank you", uncrossed her legs, stood up and reached for the pile of files and papers on the chair.

"Here, let me get those for you."

"No, really, it's all right, they're not heavy", as she struggled to side-step between the chair and his desk.

"Oh, one of those, are you? Is it all right for me to open the door for you?" as he reached for the handle and held the door open just enough for her to squeeze by.

His sarcasm still burned her ears as she quickly turned to her desk to set down her burden. The four desks in the work area across from hers were already empty, the mass migration to the coffee room being in full flow. Sharon hurried toward the soul-satisfying aroma of freshly brewed coffee and the comforting murmur of a large group of women talking and laughing behind the lunchroom door.

She entered and found herself right behind Anna in the lineup for service. She felt weak with hunger. Or was it nervous exhaustion?

"Hi Sharon, how did it go?" asked Anna, as she poured cream into her coffee.

"Oh, not too bad, I guess. My shorthand sure got a workout, though."

"You poor thing, having to use shorthand--he's such a dinosaur!." Anna walked toward the couch at the other end of the room, motioning to Sharon to join her there.

"Thanks, Anna, I'll be right there." She turned to the coffee server with a "Thank you," and was startled when her peripheral vision showed that Westbrook had just joined the coffee lineup behind her and was watching. She felt a panic in her arms as she grabbed her tray and carried it toward Anna, with the cup and saucer rattling. She begged the heavens to make sure she wouldn't stumble in her haste.

The lunch room itself was used by only the female legal assistants and office staff. For the lawyers, managers, law students and male staff members, it was the route through which they carried their snacks and coffee on their way to their own hideaway behind the heavy door with a brass name plate "Library".

Sharon was comforted to see her favorite recliner chair in the far corner of the room, remembering the lunch hour naps she had enjoyed during the months around her husband's death. Teri had taken to sitting on the couch beside her, reading a magazine and keeping the corner quiet.

Sharon knew that the law firm enjoyed a high level of employee loyalty. Its employee benefits, including the workout room and showers, were the envy of the industry. Sharon counted the lunch room as a major benefit for her and an acknowledgment of the need for a true break from the stresses of legal work.

Any of the lawyers who were brave enough to interrupt their assistants' coffee or lunch break in the lunch room were usually greeted by the amused grins of the other assistants, who generally felt that the need for urgency was only in the mind of the interrupting lawyer.

As Sharon worked her way through the six round tables surrounded by seated chatting coffee-sipping fellow assistants, she was stopped by Teri's hand on her arm.

Teri interrupted her animated conversation at her table, turning to Sharon to say "Hi there kiddo. I was going to save a chair for you but Anna said that Westbrook had you in there for nearly an hour, so I knew you'd like your "napping" corner this morning. How's it going?"

"Oh, just fine. I'll recuperate here for a few minutes before returning to the salt mine."

"That's a girl, you can do it," laughed Teri.

Sharon sank into the recliner after setting her tray on the side-table, thanking Anna for holding her place and exchanging several "good-mornings" with the other occupants of the couch and chair at her end of the room. She rested her head back and let the conversations carry on around her, occasionally nodding her awareness, but feeling the need to close her eyes for a few minutes.

The morning's announcement of a client's death had brought back Sharon's memories of the previous January, when her uncle had died.

CHAPTER 4

Desiree's pre-dawn phone call that cold January morning still echoed in her memory.

"Sharon, he's gone."

Quickly throwing her blankets back, Sharon sat up, "Oh Desi, I'm so sorry..."

"I want to go too"

Tears welled up. Sharon could feel the choking abandonment in Desi's voice, and wanted to console her. "Oh, Desi, I'm so sorry. I'll catch the next ferry, please just be calm. My poor sweetheart, I'll be there as soon as I can."

"You are my angel."

Choking back the cry aching at the back of her throat, and feeling she needed to be strong for her aunt's sake, Sharon asked "Have you called 911? Where is Uncle Donald?"

"The ambulance people took him away just now. They said it was too late." The sudden silence was broken by a wracking sob, and a wailed "I wish I could die too."

Months later, Sharon couldn't remember much about the days she had stayed with Desiree on the Island, working through all the arrangements and paperwork as if she were on automatic pilot. She had slept on the hide-a-bed in the cozy living room under several of Desi's colorful knitted afghans, waking often during the nights when she could hear Desi stirring or moaning in her sleep.

Sharon was thankful that her uncle had preplanned his estate so that no Court application or payment of Court fees would be necessary. He had transferred most of his assets into Desiree's name over the previous few years, leaving their home and bank accounts in joint ownership so that only the Death Certificate would be needed to settle his estate. Sharon had suspected that her uncle and aunt were reasonably wealthy, but when she and Desi had finished the estate paperwork, Sharon realized that Desi was now a multimillionaire.

"My goodness Desi, Uncle Donald has certainly managed things well. You won't have anything to worry about."

Tears filled Desi's eyes, "He was my hero. I would rather have him back, even if I had to be as poor as a church mouse."

Sharon could feel her throat tightening, and to avoid the tears that would follow, she jumped up, "Let's be two little church mice and have some cheese and crackers and a nice cup of tea. We've worked hard enough today, n'est pas?

Desiree smiled "You're such a sweetheart; what would I do without you?"

Sharon had been between two semesters from the University courses when her Uncle's estate was nearing completion. During that visit, she hadn't left Desi's side until they had finished all the arrangements and paperwork. A calmness had finally embraced Desi, and she had slept through the night for two nights in a row.

Finally, Sharon had realized that she had to get back to the mainland, but was wracked with guilt about leaving her aunt alone. "I'm so sorry I can't stay much longer; are you going to be okay, or would you like to come stay with me in Vancouver for a while?"

"No, I'll be fine. I'm going to keep myself busy. My neighbor Elizabeth has been very kind over the past few months, and I want to treat her to lunch at the Inn. Maybe she and I will start going to the library and the fitness center again too."

Sharon was comforted but slightly uneasy, knowing that Desi was adamant about never being a "burden" on anyone and would make herself sound more cheerful than she felt. Attempting to keep cheerful thoughts flowing, Sharon suggested "Maybe we could plan a little holiday around the end of April this year. I'll be on another break from studying then. We could think about a cruise or something, wouldn't that be fun?"

Both of them kept up their cheerful facade until they hugged goodbye, then the tears, followed by embarrassed giggles, separated them.

Sharon had waved from the car window and started her drive along the rain-slicked highway. The long highway drive through the Island forests, and the subsequent ferry ride across the stormy, dark Straights had been the loneliest she had ever experienced.

CHAPTER 5

As Sharon felt someone touch her hand, she jumped and opened her eyes. "Oh, sorry Anna, I must have been lost in thought."

"Oh, come on my dear, I heard you snoring!" laughed Anna. "Anyway, that's okay, I didn't want you to sleep past our 15-minute deadline. You looked so peaceful." She glanced at Sharon. "By the way, did Mr. Burns tell you why he needed you for Michael Westbrook?" Anna grinned, her dark brown eyes twinkling in merriment under the lush black eyelashes.

Sharon moved forward in her seat, ready to stand up. "He told me that his current secretary is on long-term sick leave, and the last temp walked out after two days. But I think my shorthand is the biggest reason he's trying me." She glanced up at Anna. "Your eyes are telling me there's some deep dark secret I should know."

"Oh, you'll find out soon enough." chuckled Anna, peering over her half-circle reading glasses and grinning at Sharon "C'mon, we'd better get back to our slave stations before our call buzzers start going off."

They both strolled out of the coffee room and along the hallway around to their work area, giggling as they discussed the hated call buzzers and where they would like to put them. The "buzzer" boxes, with their colored lights for each of the four legal assistants in each work area, were in full view from the hallways, attached at the upper corner of each alcove. Originally set up so the lawyers could easily signal for their assistants, the buzzer-and-light system became a rude demand for attention.

Although Anna joked about the buzzer, she was one of the lucky assistants who was seldom summoned by it. She had worked for her lawyer for over ten years, and he seemed to prefer the more gentle approach of either using his telephone intercom or opening his door and leaning around the corner to speak directly to Anna.

Relieved to see that her light had not been activated, Sharon turned to her desk, "I'm starting to feel like one of Pavlov's subjects again - buzzers and lights equal teeth grinding and frowns!"

Sharon's curiosity was awakened by Anna's attempt at secrecy, but she could confirm only that Westbrook had gone through two secretaries in very short order. She wanted to find out more about him, and by mid-afternoon, after his door had been closed since lunchtime, she summoned up her courage and tapped on the door before opening it a few inches to ask "May I bring you a cup of coffee?"

A look of pleasant surprise on his face, he said "No, but thanks for asking."

Closing the file in front of him, he looked up at Sharon. "While you're up, would you please see if the three articling students can come to my office at four o'clock tomorrow afternoon?"

"Do I need to tell them the purpose?" Sharon gave him a cheerful look, trying to soften her question.

"No," he frowned, "I'm their supervising lawyer. They've been waiting for my summons." He paused, a smile playing in his eyes, "Don't worry, they won't bite you."

Sharon smiled in return, shut his door, and felt the color rush to her cheeks, realizing that her heart was pounding. "Calm down, girl" she thought to herself, he probably just wants to make sure I meet the students." She walked over to Anna's desk, and bent down to whisper, "Where do I find the law students, are they still at the other end of the building in the little library?"

Anna looked up mischievously, "Are you sure you want to venture into that den, it's holding three wild ones this year, and one of them is Westbrook's son."

Sharon grinned, "Oh, thanks a lot, Anna. I'm a nervous wreck already and now I get to deal with wild things?" She straightened up. "Anyway, I've been directed to round them up for Westbrook. I don't know why he can't just telephone them himself."

Anna's dark eyes twinkled, her long false eyelashes almost touching the upper rim of her glasses as she winked, "Maybe he's just testing you."

Sharon picked up her notebook and pencil off her desk, took a deep breath, and headed toward the far end of the building, to the small library. The door was shut, and she imagined the three students on the other side of the door would be heads down over books and notes.

She knocked on the door, opened it a crack. "Hi folks, may I enter?" She opened the door wide and was surprised to discover two of them convulsed in laughter on either side of the long conference table which dominated the room.

As she entered the room, the third student jumped down off the library ladder leaning against the book shelves at the back of the room and straightened his jacket.

Sharon looked directly at the tall, broad-shouldered jumper, who appeared to be the dominant actor in the room. "You must be David, you look so much like your father. I hope I'm not interrupting something important?"

"Your smile tells me you already know the answer. You're Sharon, right?" as he walked past his audience and toward Sharon.

"Yes. Mr. Westbrook has asked that all three of you meet in his office tomorrow afternoon at four. Can I tell him you'll be there?"

"Whoa, all business here! Could we start with a little 'Hello, how are you?' instead?"

Reaching out while Sharon fumbled her book and pen before shaking his hand, David announced, "I am David Westbrook, and pleased to meet you." Pointing to his audience, he continued, "And this is Jenny Carson, who is going to save the world, and over there is Ravi Singh, our referee and calming influence."

Sharon smiled weakly "Nice to meet all of you, I'm sorry to interrupt."

David let go of Sharon's hand, and playfully saluted Sharon. "Since I'm at least 10 years older than my fellow students, we've all agreed that I can lead the charge. I'll make sure we get there tomorrow, and if I don't Jenny will break my arm."

Jenny rolled her eyes, then nodded a smiling farewell as Sharon turned to the door.

The rest of that afternoon Sharon spent at her desk, taking only a quick break to gulp down an iced tea drink. At the end of the day, after organizing her desk and materials for the next day, she was just pulling her purse out of the bottom drawer, ready to leave, when the call buzzer sounded. Looking up she could see it was Westbrook's light flashing at her.

Surprised that she was being called at this late hour, she opened the door enough to stick her head in, asking "Do I need to bring my notebook?"

"No, this will just take a few minutes. Come in and sit down." He motioned toward the front of his desk and waited for Sharon to settle into the chair closest to the door. "Thank you for rounding up the students for me. I'll want you to sit in on the meeting with them tomorrow, with your notebook." He looked up at her, a small grin showing at the side of his mouth. "Do you mind if I call you by your first name?"

Wide-eyed with surprise, Sharon could feel her heart thumping. "No, not at all."

"That's good. One of the things I don't like about this place is the formality of calling everyone by their surnames. I want you to stop calling me sir, and use my first name, Michael."

"Thank you Mr. Westbr..."

"Michael, remember?" He lowered his eyes to his hands, folded in front of him on the desk. "I won't be in the office until about noon tomorrow, so I want you to open all my mail, pile the urgent letters and documents in date order with their files attached, and prepare draft replies to any routine matters."

"Sure, will do." Sharon watched as he turned his attention to dialing the phone. Feeling dismissed, she stood up and walked back to her desk. "Well, he sure runs hot and cold." Sharon frowned as she and Anna walked down the hall. "Now I must call him Michael, but he still treats me like furniture."

"Welcome to the club" grinned Anna, "You might want to take up drinking."

"Thank heavens this day is over", thought Sharon, almost wishing she were a drinker.

Teri, standing at her reception desk as they turned into the waiting room, called out, "Hey, Sharon, would you like a drive to your place, like old times?"

"Oh, thank you, Teri, you're a doll. Just let me get my coat."

As Sharon and Anna walked through the elevator hallway, Anna remarked, "Teri amazes me, I don't know where she gets her energy."

"She is a little ball of fire, isn't she?" Sharon smiled, "She's been wonderful to me and she's really good at calming me down. We spend most of the time laughing when she's driving me home."

Within minutes, Sharon was relaxed in Teri's compact car, amused to see that Teri still leaned forward over the steering wheel while she drove.

Teri glanced at Sharon. "Well, kiddo, how did it go today?"

"My head is spinning, I don't know what to think of Westbrook. One minute I think he wants to get rid of me, and the next he's wanting us to go on a first-name basis."

"Don't worry, you're the perfect person for that spot right now. Michael is currently in a battle of egos with Hird, and having the city's best legal assistant there is just what Michael needs."

"You're joking. Quit that!" laughed Sharon.

"I hear you had to round up the students for a meeting. What did you think of Michael's son, David?"

"I'm amazed. I had no idea he even had a son. Where has Michael been hiding him?"

"David was brought up by Michael's first wife back in Ottawa. Went to boarding school, earned scholarships galore, got a degree in marine biology of all things. Apparently he spent the last three years before law school traveling all over the world on his yacht."

"You continue to amaze me, Teri, how do you manage to hear about all that stuff?"

"Aha, I'll never tell" laughed Teri, her bracelets jangling as she raced around a corner on an amber light, while Sharon's right foot pushed the phantom passenger brake to the floor.

Taking a breath to calm her voice, Sharon said "He's quite the looker. Is he married?"

"Funny you should ask." chuckled Teri, "I've heard through the grapevine that Michael is pressuring him to settle down, especially now that he's moved to Vancouver, and has his law degree. Michael doesn't want David to repeat his mistakes."

"Mistakes?" asked Sharon.

"Well, like failing at marriage and having to share the family fortune."

Sharon looked out the window. "Oh darn, we're at my place already. I'm dying to hear more about this family. Oh, that reminds me, you'll probably be seeing the cutest little French lady some time in the next couple of weeks, my aunt, Desiree. You'll know her right away, she has curly white hair and the sweetest accent you've every heard, and she loves wearing hats."

Teri smiled, "I'll keep my eyes open for her! See you tomorrow."

CHAPTER 6

The next day Sharon, enjoying the freedom and responsibility, opened Westbrook's mail, scribbled out a list of files to be pulled, and walked down the hall to the central filing room. Standing at the counter, noticing the filing clerk's quizzical look, she smiled, "Hi, I'm Sharon, working for Michael Westbrook. Could these files be delivered to his office as soon as possible?"

Rolling her eyes, the filing clerk grinned, "As usual, in a big hurry."

"I'm sorry," Sharon smiled in return, "I'm just trying to make a good impression for my second day on the job."

"Oh, you lucky thing, how long do you think you'll last?"

Eyebrows raised, her smile fading, Sharon murmured, "I'll be fine. I'm pretty stubborn."

"You may as well take this pile of files back with you. These are all his bring-forward files for today. I'll be down with these other files in a few minutes."

Looking up from the name plate on the counter, Sharon said "Thank you, Carol" as she picked up the foot-high pile of legal files and turned toward the hallway.

Later that afternoon, just before the appointed hour, Sharon saw the three law students appear at the far end of the hallway. Sharon watched as they walked toward her. Jenny Carson in the lead position of the trio, her red, shoulder-length fly-away hair bouncing on her shoulders with each step, was followed by David and Ravi, both of them smiling down at the serious determination stomping ahead of them. "Hi gang," smiled Sharon as they approached her desk, "Just give me a minute to see if Mr. Westbrook is ready. We'll also need to roll my chair into his office."

Michael Westbrook didn't look up as his son, David, rolled Sharon's chair to the far back corner of the room while the other students settled themselves into the chairs facing his desk. Sharon sat down where her chair had been put, wondering whether David wanted her to be closer to the window, or just out of the way. "Probably like father, like son," thought Sharon, as she watched Michael stand up, turn to the window and stand looking at the harbor below, apparently lost in thought.

The three students, with David in the middle, shifted in their chairs, questioning looks passing between them. David finally shrugged and cleared his throat, ready to speak. "Um, .."

Michael turned toward the students. Sharon saw Jenny jump as Michael's loud "Okay," put a sudden stop to the nervous anticipation bouncing among the three of them. Michael sat down and put his forearms on his desk, looking directly at each of them in turn.

"You are all here to take on an estate file." Michael glanced at David's upraised eyebrows. "Yes, I'm not the estate lawyer, but you will be reporting to me."

David sat forward, "But Dad.."

"Let me finish, then you can ask questions." Michael opened the file on his desk. Picking up the yellow foolscap sheet, he announced, "The lady who died on Sunday, Mary Boyle, was a very wealthy, very important client of the firm. Mr. Fisher prepared her Will several years ago, and it appoints Fisher as her Executor, and gives most of her estate to charities."

With his elbows on his desk, Michael turned the yellow foolscap sheet, covered with Fisher's handwritten notes, to let it hang from his fingertips, facing his audience. "You will see that Fisher is very thorough with these things, and you'll find all the information to start the estate process right here."

He turned the sheet again, reviewing the notes for a few seconds. "It looks like her original Will is being kept in our vault." He lay the sheet down, rolled his chair away from the desk and stood up. "I'm going to tell you the first three steps you must take before anything else is done, and after that you're on your own."

He turned to glance out his window, pausing at the view of the mountains, before continuing. "I don't want you taking the easy way out by getting precedents from the estate secretaries."

Turning to Sharon, "I want you to contact the word-processing girls, Fisher's assistant, and that other assistant who does Wills and estates, and let them know they can't help the students."

Sharon asked, "Does that mean I can't help them either?"

Michael replied, "Absolutely. I want these three to dig out the law books and procedure manuals and work through the process on their own. The only thing you're allowed to do is type out any letters and documents that they have prepared, mistakes and all. I'll read the stuff and go over it with them to suggest changes." Then with a grin, he added, "or destroy it, as the case may be."

Sharon saw the looks that passed among the three, all hesitant to ask any questions.

Michael turned to face them again, "So, the very first thing is to get an original death certificate and start the funeral process. Once the certificate is in, you'll order a Wills Search from the Division of Vital Statistics, to confirm that Mrs. Boyle's didn't sign any other Wills. The Will we did for her must be the last will she signed before she died."

He flipped over a couple of papers in the file, then glanced at Jenny as she leaned over her knee to scribble onto her notepad. "You won't need to secure her residence because she has been in a care home for the past few years, and they have padlocked her room. You'll find papers in this file showing that she had prearranged and prepaid her funeral services. You'll need to contact the funeral company. They will pick up her remains once the coroner releases them."

David broke the ensuing silence, asking "You want all three of us to work on this together?"

"Yes, David, I do" said Michael firmly, "I want this to be a joint effort. You can decide among the three of you how. None of you is to act unilaterally. If one of you knows for certain what needs doing, you'll discuss it with the other two so that I can ask any one of you at any time, and you'll all be up to speed on the file's progress. Any more questions?"

Jenny, turning in her chair to face the door, used the back of her hand to push her hair back from her eyes and looked directly at David and Ravi, who were both putting their pens in their shirt pockets. Leaning forward to get out of her chair, she announced "Well, I'm okay for now, how about you guys?"

David stood up, "If we have questions after we've done our research..."

"You'll come to me," interrupted Michael as he walked to the door. "If I'm tied up, Sharon is your only other source. She'll be keeping track of your questions too." He opened the door, and waved them out before he walked toward Sharon's chair.

"I'll roll it back." Sharon jumped up and grabbed for the back of her chair, almost stepping on his foot, "Oh, I'm sorry..."

"Calm down, my dear, I can roll a chair."

CHAPTER 7

That first week in the office flew by. Sharon settled into a comfortable but rushed routine, falling into her old habit of almost running when she walked down the hallways. After her time spent in casual jeans, sweaters and sneakers at the University, she almost resented having to fit into the "legal assistant" look by wearing skirts or dresses, pantyhose and heels. She could feel her growing urge to escape fueling her ambition to operate her own law office with her own look and rules.

Now it was Friday and she needed to rush home to change, pick up her suitcase and drive to the ferry terminal for the trip to the Island. She wasn't certain she could catch the seven o'clock ferry without speeding, but knew it wouldn't matter much anyway, as she had prepared to spend the first night at her favorite Inn on the Island. She had explained to the reservations clerk that she might be arriving as late as eleven o'clock in the evening, depending on which ferry she could catch.

The quiet, old-fashioned Inn had been where she and her late husband had enjoyed their last few days together before he went into hospice. It held bittersweet but comforting memories for her as it had been their last refuge from reality. The only reality they had not been able to avoid was the regular dose of morphine she had to administer to him.

They had made frequent use of the room service for their evening meals, choosing to sit on the room's third-floor balcony to look out over the water and watch the shadows creep up the mountains on the other side of the Straights as the sun moved below the horizon behind them.

Sharon, having parked her car on the upper car deck of the ferry, took the escalator to the passenger deck to settle in for the relaxing two-hour ferry trip to the Island. Her face still held the smile that had appeared when the traffic flagman had waved her and the car behind her onto the seven o'clock ferry. They had been the two last ferry customers allowed to board before the ramps were hoisted up.

As Sharon reached the top of the escalator, the heavy vibration of the ship as it pulled away from the dock, confirmed her belief that her boarding had been last-minute good luck. The ferry was already on its way. She knew she could reach the Inn, just a short drive up the east coast of the Island, in time to phone her Aunt, then enjoy a leisurely bubble bath in the big iron claw-foot tub.

On the ferry, she had been able to find a seat by the window on the upper passenger deck, to take advantage of the remaining daylight and watch the sunset. The mild vibration of the huge diesel engines as they settled into cruising speed brought a soothing loosening of Sharon's tense shoulder and neck muscles, as she watched the ship pull further out into the harbor.

The evening sun was painting a warm glow on the dark rock wall which loomed over the harbor, and she turned in her seat to watch the shore disappear behind her as the ship turned westward toward the Island. Through the windows on the far side of the ship, Sharon watched as the next ferry passed by on its way to the harbor, getting ready to spit out its load of cars, trucks, buses and passengers.

Sharon loved being on the water, feeling the movement of the waves, filling her lungs with the fresh sea air. It reminded her of all her childhood summer holidays, spent cruising around the Gulf Islands and up the Straights in her parents' boat.

Her seat was close enough to the cafeteria for the enticing odor of hamburgers and fries to tickle her nostrils, making her realize she was actually very hungry. She disliked line-ups of any kind, so waited until the mass of hungry passengers had finally moved to their seats before she walked to the glass-fronted shelves with a tray. Her mouth watered as she picked out a salad and dessert, then ordered a bowl of clam chowder and a dinner bun from the cook. She had always enjoyed the food service on the ferries, in spite of her friends' negative comparison to "airplane food".

Every time she took a ferry ride, she enjoyed the feeling that she was now on a holiday, making everything taste that much better. Maybe it was the ocean atmosphere, or maybe it was just because she wasn't doing the cooking, she wasn't sure, but she enjoyed the delicious experience.

Soon after finishing her dinner, Sharon heard the announcement blaring for all passengers to proceed to the vehicle decks to prepare for disembarking. Sharon remained relaxed in her cushioned vinyl seat, waiting for the crushing crowd to disappear down the escalators and stairs before she got up to travel down to her car on the deck below.

Pulling into the parking area behind the ocean-front Inn, Sharon felt the little jump of excitement as she admired the quaint Victorian-style structure, with its white stucco and dark brown wood framework surrounding the leaded glass windows and entry doors. She grabbed her suitcase from the trunk of her car and hurried into the lobby.

Soon afterward she turned the key into her room at the Inn, stepped inside and took a long satisfying breath. She had managed to reserve the very room that she and her husband had enjoyed on their last trip together, hoping that somehow coming back to that room might remind her of how strong she could be.

She opened the french doors to the balcony. Stepping outside to look at the shore she lifted her head up and took a deep breath. The fresh ocean air cooled her body and soothed her mind. The last of the evening's twilight glow was fading, and she could see a few stars twinkling above her.

Suddenly remembering that she had promised to phone Desi, Sharon returned to the room and sat down at the roll-top desk. "Hi Desi, it's me. I'm at the Inn now. How are you?"

"My sweetheart, it's so good to hear your voice and know you are close by."

"I'll probably get to your place tomorrow morning around ten, if that's not too early?"

"No, of course not. I can hardly wait, and you know me. I'm such an early bird."

Sharon and Desi chatted for a few more minutes, and after she had put down the phone, she sat looking around the room. The cool evening breeze had started to move the lacy sheer curtains at the french doors, and the puffy white comforter folded at the foot of the four-poster bed looked inviting.

Sharon kicked off her shoes, turned on the bedside Tiffany lamp, and rolled onto the bed as she grabbed the comforter to cover her legs. She leaned back against the pillows she had piled up against the headboard and propped her book up on her knees. She was glad to have some quiet time to unwind from that first crazy week at the office, hoping to be well-rested for the 2-hour drive tomorrow morning.

She set her alarm for seven so that she would be awake around sunrise to see how the day looked. After taking one last step out onto the balcony she came inside and closed the french doors before tying back the curtains in front of them. She wanted to be able to see the ocean and the sky in the morning from her bed.

The next morning the sun woke her before the alarm rang, and through her squinting eyes she could see there was just enough cloud above the distant mountains to give the sunrise a blazing red start.

She bunched her pillows behind her head and watched the brightness intensify and broaden, as the sun rose through the morning cloud, sending hazy rays of white brightness to bounce off the ocean and into her room. The watery reflected sunlight fluttered over the ceiling and the bed canopy above her, and for a while she lay back to watch the dancing lights, before she finally stretched, threw back the silky sheets and comforter, and rolled to the side of her bed.

"Darn, I should have worn something to bed last night" she thought as she crouched her way to the french doors to loosen and close the curtains before standing up to get dressed. She couldn't help laughing at herself, remembering her late husband's chuckle as he had teased her, "Don't be silly, no one is going to see you in here, unless there's some pervert with a telescope over on the mainland."

Feeling refreshed and happy about the weekend ahead of her, Sharon trotted down two flights of the wide stone stairway in the middle of the Inn, to enjoy the free continental breakfast and rich steaming coffee set out in the small dining room. She waved a good morning to the elderly couple sipping their coffee at one of the tables by the waterfront windows, then sat down to scan the daily newspaper that had been abandoned at a small round table in the center.

A few minutes later after checking her watch, she jumped up realizing that she should be on the road to her Aunt's cottage right away, if she wanted to enjoy the drive and avoid speeding.

In her room, she threw a few dollar bills on the dresser as a tip for the room staff. A sigh escaped her mouth as she took one last wistful look around the room before grabbing her suitcase and running out to her car.

She had always loved the leisurely two-hour drive from the Inn to her Uncle's cottage, especially when the weather was warm enough for her to leave her windows down. The cool air calmed her as she drove through the small beach tourist towns, with their flower-lined streets and lamp-posts heavy with hanging flower baskets.

Soon she reached the section of the highway that was heavily forested on each side. On her right she passed driveway entrances and signs of habitation interrupting the forest density.

The variety of signs made her smile, as she admired the creativity of the residents in identifying their driveways. The houses in this area were on the waterfront edge of large parcels of land, most hidden out of view from the highway through the trees. Some of the decorated mailboxes, twisted driftwood creatures and carved wooden address signs had been in place for years, making it easy to see when a home had changed owners and adopted a new identity at its entry from the highway.

As she neared the northern end of the forested area Sharon flipped on her car's right turn signal and slowed down as she recognized the familiar signs of her Aunt's neighbors.

The highway had originally been a simple two-lane country road running behind the waterfront lots, but as traffic and population grew, the country road was transformed into a raised, 4-lane highway. The entrances to the waterfront properties were widened and built up to gradually slope up to the shoulder of the new highway, but left unpaved.

Sharon had always felt a little nervous entering her Uncle's driveway, afraid she might slide down on the gravel. In spite of her late husband's teasing, she had always flipped on her turn signal far before she reached the entrance, wanting to provide plenty of time for the following drivers to avoid her.

She turned down into the driveway, which was still shaded from the early morning sun. That familiar little jump of anticipation tickled her stomach as she drove through the trees on the narrow rutted road toward the cottage.

Years ago her Uncle had cleared a large area directly behind the cottage to build a 2-car garage and lay down a large area of colorful patio bricks between the garage and the south edge of the cottage. Large ceramic buckets full of colorful flowers were spaced along the front of the patio, and the large burl coffee table in the center was surrounded by four white wicker chairs with teal-blue tufted soft seat cushions. Sharon could feel the welcoming warmth of the scene as she walked to the back door, which she found locked.

Her rata-tat-tat knock on the door produced no response, and the garage window to her left showed no sign of life inside. She walked across the patio to the pathway leading to the front of the house.

Passing the chimney for the fireplace, Sharon couldn't help but look up to admire the creative handiwork of her Uncle. He had added the fireplace and built the chimney himself, using colorful, rounded rocks that he and Desi had gathered on their travels around the Island. Desi had so loved that stone-decorated chimney that she had built a garden around the base of it and filled it with flowers and ferns.

Knowing that Desi's hearing had deteriorated slightly, Sharon called "Desi, I'm here, where are you?", as she rounded the corner of the sunny front porch. She couldn't help laughing as she saw Desi quickly look up from her bent-over position, several white curls falling into her eyes.

Desi used the back of her garden-gloved hand to push back the curls and waved at Sharon. Desi's love of color, as always, had influenced her wardrobe choices of that morning. A bright red scarf tied back most of her hair, and Donald's purple-flowered Hawaiian shirt hung loosely over the black, baggy cotton trousers she had tucked into her red galoshes, which were folded down, Musketeer-style.

"You're here already" cried Desi, her bright smile contrasting with her flushed face as she threw down the trowel and rushed to Sharon. "I'm so glad to see you"

"Me too. I got up early this morning and the drive was easy."

"Is it ten already? I must have lost track of time."

They hugged each other, then walked up onto the front porch where Desi sat down on the wicker bench seat to slip off her galoshes.

"The yard looks so pretty, you've been working too hard, I think"

"Oh, you know me, I love being outside, and the exercise is good for me."

"You're such an inspiration," sighed Sharon as she walked toward the front door. "Shall I put the kettle on for us? Would you like some tea?"

"Thank you, dear. That would be lovely. I'll just go wash up and then I'll get out the butter tarts I made for us"

"Oh yummy, I can hardly wait."

Sharon and Desi settled into their easy-going, comfortable companionship, sipping their tea from Desi's colorful fine English china cups. Quiet moments had them both gazing out the large living-room windows to watch the long branches of the willow tree at the front fence swing in the breeze. Desi put her hand to her forehead as if to shade her eyes, "I see whitecaps on the water out there, I hope we're not going to have a storm."

"We'll be fine. All the tall trees around us keep it pretty sheltered in here."

"Yes, you're right. I shouldn't worry. Maybe it will be more calm tomorrow."

"There were a few whitecaps on the water last night, but the trip was nice. The weather has to be really fierce before they'll cancel any ferry sailings."

"What time will we leave tomorrow?" Desi reached to pick up the now-empty plate of goodies, "Maybe I should be getting busy with my packing."

"I'll help, Desi. Here, let me do the dishes," Sharon cleared the table, then returned to her chair, "and I don't want us to forget anything before we leave for Vancouver." She pulled a pen and small writing pad from her purse,

"I'm going to make a list, so we won't need to worry."

CHAPTER 8

Monday morning, walking back from the filing room to her desk, laden with yet another pile of bring-forward files, Sharon was ready to turn into her alcove when Anna leaned over and called, "You should have seen the cute little old lady Mr. Fisher had in his..."

"Has she already left?" interrupted Sharon. "Oh my gosh, that was fast."

Anna pointed down the hall toward the reception area, "I think she just turned the corner at the end of the hall."

Sharon dumped the files on the side of her desk and ran down the hallway and through Teri's reception area. "Desi!" she called as she saw Fisher and Desi in conversation in front of the elevators. Rushing over to them, she said, "Excuse me, Mr. Fisher" as she turned to Desi, "I'm sorry I missed you, I was in the file room when you came."

"There you are, my dear!" Desi smiled as she turned to Sharon. "Mr. Fisher has asked me to come back before lunch to sign everything. Maybe we can go out for lunch when he's finished?"

"That will work out fine for me, I can take my lunch break whenever you're ready."

Desi turned to Fisher, "Shall I come back ten minutes before noon?"

Fisher looked surprised that he was again part of the conversation. "Oh, yes. That will be good. We should only need a few minutes after you've read through your Will."

"Okay, I'll scoot away until then."

Surprised at Desi's determination to leave, Sharon asked, "Where are you going until then?"

Desi turned to whisper to Sharon, "I'll just go do a bit of shopping in that underground Mall up the street." Turning again to wave at Fisher as he walked away, Desi called out "Thank you, Mr. Fisher."

Sharon bent down to hug her Aunt, "Okay, sweetie, have fun. We'll see you later."

As Sharon walked back to her desk, she grinned as she remembered her aunt's statement yesterday, while they were driving off the ferry. "I phoned your office last week and made an appointment to see Mr. Fisher."

"You did?" Sharon had asked, her eyes wide with pleased amazement as she had glanced at her Aunt and seen her determined look and happy smile.

Dennis Fisher was back in his office well before Sharon had returned to her desk. She had no sooner settled in her chair when he emerged from his office and handed Sharon a thin file folder with a yellow foolscap sheet, covered with his hand-written notes, attached to the front cover. "Say kiddo, could you do me a great favor. Your sweet little French friend wants just a very straight-forward Will, and Betty has enough other work to do right now."

Before Sharon could mention that Desi was her late uncle's wife, Fisher went on to summarize his notes. "Just do the usual simple Will, you know, standard revocation clause, pay debts, etcetera. She wants everything to go to these two charities" as he pointed to the yellow sheet. "Oh, and don't forget to do a Wills Notice for filing with Vital Statistics."

Sharon wondered why Fisher hadn't asked his own secretary to do the job. While she had been listening to Fisher's instructions, she had noticed his secretary at her desk, right across the hall from Sharon's, lighting a cigarette.

Waiting for a few minutes after Fisher had disappeared into his office, Sharon approached Betty's desk asking, "Betty do you have some Will paper and Wills Notices handy? It would save me having to walk all the way over to the supply room and hunt for the stuff, especially since this Will has to be done right away."

"Sure, here", as she opened her desk's side drawer, "and here's the blue backing cover for the Will and the special envelope we use too."

"Thank you so much, Betty," Sharon touched Betty's shoulder, glad to see the hint of a smile on her face, "You're a dear."

Betty shook her head, "Dennis makes me so mad when he does that, tells people that we can have the darn thing ready right away. I've complained about these rush jobs - I guess that's why he asked you to do it. Give it to me, if you like, and I'll do it."

"No, that's okay" replied Sharon. "I really don't mind. I've just run out of things to do myself while Westbrook is away on that long trial. Westbrook probably told Fisher that I would have some free time this morning. Anyway I once worked for Fisher for a few weeks, and I think I remember the way he likes his Wills prepared."

"He doesn't even read them, believe me."

"Yes, I know. Dumps the pressure on us."

"Good, you know the routine."

Sharon shuffled the papers in her arms as she turned toward her desk, "I'll work from the sample Will that's in the system. What's the name of the file again?"

Betty pulled a heavy binder out of the cabinet beside her and plopped it on her desk. Pulling the folder open by one of its inside tabs, she pointed, "There, use that one" and turned it toward Sharon.

Sharon bent to read the name, then returned to her own desk. Her fingers flew over the keyboard as she hunched over Fisher's notes, determined to be finished in the event Westbrook's trial adjourned early for lunch. About an hour later, she had assembled all the documents in a file, which she took into Fisher's office, putting the file on his desk with a satisfied sigh, "There you go, all done."

"Great, you're a miracle worker! Would you go get the dear old thing for me. She's probably back in the waiting room by now."

"By the way, we're related, sort of."

"Oh, she didn't mention any blood relatives."

"Well, she married my Uncle Donald, so I'm not a blood relative, but we are very close."

"Okay, I'll get Betty to be the other witness on her Will then."

"Probably a good idea."

Sharon smiled as she walked into the reception room. "Hi sweetie, we're all ready for you now."

"My goodness what wonderful service! He's ready for me to sign things?"

"Yes, that's why I'm here, Mr. Fisher is waiting for us." Sharon reached to support Desi's elbow as she stood up from the deep-cushioned leather armchair. They walked slowly back through the office, after Teri and Sharon had shared a quick wink of acknowledgment, Sharon's smile signifying, "Yes, this is her. Isn't she cute?"

"I'm so glad we're getting this done, it is such a relief."

"I've made a reservation for our lunch when you're finished with Mr. Fisher. There's a lovely French restaurant just around the corner."

"Ooh, I can hardly wait," Desiree's clear blue eyes shining up at Sharon.

"Well, here we are. Mr. Fisher, Mrs. Dunsmore is ready to sign her Will now."

Fisher stood up to bring Desiree to the armchair in front of his desk, gently asking "Can we get you a coffee or anything while you're reading over your Will?"

"Thank you so much Mr. Fisher. No coffee for me, Sharon and I will be going out for lunch right after we're finished."

He handed the unsigned document to Desi, saying "Now, Mrs. Dunsmore, I want you to take your time to read over your Will before you sign it, and to let us know if there are any changes needed or if you have any questions. Sharon will be able to make any changes right away."

Smiling up at Sharon, Desiree said "I knew she was smart. She's going to be a lawyer, you know." Turning to the papers in front of her, she said "I don't need to read my Will, I'm certain it is fine."

Sharon could feel an embarrassed glow climbing up her face; she hadn't made it generally known to anyone in the office except Teri that she was half way to obtaining her law degree.

Fisher, obviously surprised at the maternal affection in Desiree's statement, didn't miss a beat, but insisted that Desiree take the time to read her Will anyway. "Sharon, please take Mrs. Dunsmore's ID and make photocopies of them for our file. Give us a few minutes before you ask Betty to come in with her pen and name stamp, and we can be all finished before lunch."

Sharon hurried out to the photocopy room, and as she was returning to Fisher's office she recognized the familiar spiel he spouted to most of his Wills clients, "Now you see, whenever someone prepares a Will, it is a good safety feature to send this Wills Notice to the Provincial Vital Statistics branch. That way a permanent record is kept that you've made a Will and where you plan to keep it. That's why we needed your birth date and birthplace, so that there is no question that it is your Will. We'll also be keeping photocopies of your identification documents, and taking a snapshot of you to be kept in our file, as additional evidence of your identity."

"My goodness, Mr. Fisher, you are so careful..." started Desiree, as she picked up the pen.

"Whoops, don't sign yet, Mrs. Dunsmore.." He touched her hand. " We need another witness in here with us." He turned to Sharon, "Okay, Sharon, please ask Betty to come in now."

Desi smiled "Oh my, this is all so serious."

Fisher continued his recital, "Well we can never be too careful, with all the identity theft that's happening these days. We'll keep your ID documents in our vault with a copy of your Will, so everything will be very safe."

"Yes, that seems a very sensible idea." agreed Desiree.

Desi sat forward in her chair and placed her Will on the desk, then slowly and painstakingly signed her initials at the bottom of the first pages of her Will and her full signature on the last page. She took careful notice as Fisher and Betty placed their initials and signatures as witnesses. "My goodness, such a lot of writing for one little Will. I must be very careful to put my Will into my bank as soon as I get home."

"Here Sharon, would you mind making a photocopy of the Will." He turned toward Desi. "Mrs. Dunsmore, would you like to have any extra copies of your Will to give to anyone?"

"Maybe one copy for me to keep at home, that would be good." answered Desi.

Sharon picked up Desi's Will as Fisher reached into the cabinet behind his chair and turned to Desiree with a camera in his hand, smiling, "Okay my pretty lady, please take off your hat, and give me a big smile."

Desiree giggled as she grabbed her beret from her head and used her other hand to pat down her white curls, "Oh dear, I must look a sight." She sat up straight in her chair, leaning slightly forward as she took a big breath, "Okay, cheeeese."

Sharon, still smiling about the scene in Fisher's office, rushed to the photocopy station, wondering about the new procedure of photographs at Stewart & Company. None of the other offices where she had done her temporary assignments had taken that extra step.

She returned to Fisher's office a few minutes later with the Will and several photocopies, and seeing that Desiree was gathering up her bags in readiness to leave, hurried out to her own desk. Grabbing her purse, she called out to Anna and Julia, "See you in an hour," and stood watching Fisher's door.

Fisher and Desi emerged into the hallway. Fisher held Desi's hand in both of his, bowing his head toward her, "My precious Mrs. Dunsmore, it has been my pleasure to meet you."

"Thank you so much, Mr. Fisher. I am very happy to meet you too."

Sharon stepped up behind Desiree, saying "Here I am, I..."

"Oh, you were behind me, I didn't know where your desk was." They walked together down toward the front of the office. "I was going to sit in the waiting room and ask that nice receptionist to tell you where I was."

As they turned into the waiting room, Desi gave a little wave to Teri.

Sharon steered Desi toward the armchair that was closest to Teri's switchboard desk. She whispered to Desi, "I'll just go get my coat and tidy up a bit. Then we'll toddle out for our lunch."

Teri stood up, put her forearms on the counter in front of her, bracelets clanging against the wood, and asked cheerfully "There now, are you all finished, Mrs. Dunsmore"

"Yes, I feel much better now, having that business finished. It was more expensive than I expected, but it's worth it. Mr. Fisher is so smart."

"I know, these lawyers can sometimes shock us with their bills, but as you say, it's usually worth it for the peace of mind."

"I'm going out for lunch with Sharon. She's just like her uncle, my dear departed Donald. I don't know what I'd do without her."

Teri smiled, "Sharon's pretty special here too. She told me about your cozy home, right by the water?"

"Yes, I love the ocean, it makes me feel peaceful."

Seeing Sharon returning through the elevator lobby, Teri remarked "Oh, here she is now, looking like she's hungry, as usual." As she sat down behind her counter, Teri waved a goodbye, calling "Have a great lunch, you two."

Slightly breathless, Sharon said "Away we go. We'll have lots of time to walk to the restaurant. It has a beautiful view of the harbor."

As they crossed the intersection with the early lunch crowd and walked down the street to the restaurant, Sharon shortened the pace of her usual long-legged walk to compensate for Desiree's dainty steps, while Desi's tiny hand rested inside Sharon's elbow. Sharon loved watching as passersby took extra notice of Desi, her pale mauve gloves matching the beret slanted toward her left ear atop her white curls.

At lunch, Desiree giggled as the waiter hovered over her and, in French, described the daily specials and bowed to take his leave. Sharon could understand some of their conversation, enjoying the girlish delight that Desi was taking in all the attention being shown to her.

As they sat together over their dessert and coffee, Desi's blue eyes lit up, "It is so exciting to be in the downtown. I would like to stay down here for a while and travel home with you after work. Could we do that?"

"Are you sure you won't get too tired?"

"Well, you know I love shopping." She grinned at Sharon, "and you and I both know how to shop 'til we drop." She paused for a moment, "If I need a rest, I could spend some time in that big library down the street. It's such an interesting building, don't you think?"

"What a good idea. Yes, I think the building even won some awards. I haven't taken the time to visit it yet, I'd love to hear what you think of it."

"That's what I'll do then."

"The only library I've been in lately is the Law Library, and it has no style at all."

Desi laughed, "Well, I'll avoid the Law Library then."

"If you could be back in the office around 4:30, you could relax in the reception area until we're all ready to go. We'll be getting a ride from Teri."

They finished their coffee and at the door their waiter met them and took Desiree's hand, bowing to kiss it, "Madam, it has been my pleasure to meet you. I hope you have a wonderful day."

Sharon smiled at both of them as Desiree shyly giggled her thanks.

Outside, they hugged each other, before Sharon turned back toward the office.

CHAPTER 9

Sharon got back to her desk just before Westbrook returned from his lunch. Although they had been working together for a week, she still couldn't think of him as a "Michael." Her years of working in law offices had brain-washed her into thinking in formal terms only. Besides, she was still too ill-at-ease with him to call him Michael, and simply started every new conversation with "Excuse me, but.."

Westbrook appeared in the hallway, but didn't acknowledge seeing Sharon until he was passing her desk. Pausing to bend toward her, he said in a quiet voice, "Hello Sharon, could you bring your book in, please?"

Sharon grabbed her notebook and pencils and stepped through his door as he rolled his chair to sit down.

"Just sit down for now, no dictation yet. I want to ask you a few things."

"Oh-oh," thought Sharon, "This must be the part that scares off secretaries." She plunked herself into the chair, and leaning toward him, she looked warily into his eyes.

"First of all, how long can I expect you to stay here?"

Taken aback, Sharon said "I'll be available until the end of June, if Mr. Burns wants me to stay that long."

"What happens in July?"

"I've agreed to do a three-week assignment for another firm."

"Do you do this all the time, a few weeks here and there?"

"I have been for the past three years; I'm also taking some University courses, so I need a fair bit of time off."

"Sounds like you're trying to do it all. Why don't you work for one office on a part-time basis instead of flitting around like a butterfly?"

Sharon thought, "Easy for you to say, just try to find a job like that", then, straightening her back and lifting her chin said "I just haven't found the right job yet."

"Or you just haven't found the right man yet?" he asked sarcastically.

Sharon's hands tightened on her book and pencils as she stood up, reddening, and turned toward the door.

He jumped up from his chair, and almost shouted "Okay, I'm sorry, sit down."

Sharon didn't try to hide the anger in her eyes, as she leaned back into her chair and looked, unsmiling, into his face. He swiveled his chair back and forth for a few minutes before coming to a stop facing the window.

It was a good opportunity for Sharon to note his profile - high forehead with prominent brows, deep-set brooding eyes, long straight nose, gray hair showing at his temples, combed back to end in soft waves of thick, light-brown hair at the back of his neck. "How can such good looks harbor such nastiness?" she thought to herself.

He turned to pick up a pencil from his desk, and before he swiveled back to face the view of the Vancouver harbor, gently tapping the eraser end on his chin, he took a quick glance at Sharon. Frowning slightly, he took a deep breath and started "Look, it's like this, I want a secretary I can count on for a long time. My first secretary up and left last year because her husband's job changed, and the one after her is now on sick leave which I think she'll milk for all its worth. The last few that Burns came up with just didn't take enough responsibility for their job."

"From what I've seen so far, and from what Burns told me, I think you may be just what I've been looking for. Would you consider settling with one job if you were given enough time off?"

Sharon was so surprised by his conciliatory attitude that she couldn't think of any good answer. She had worked with him for such a short time, and right from the first she had felt on edge. "That depends." Taking a long breath, she said "I'm not sure I can keep up with all your work on a part-time basis, you've been so busy."

He laughed, "Well, you're the first decent secretary I've had for nearly a year. I've been limping along with the bodies they've been sending me, so you and I have been dealing with a big back-log."

Sharon thought for a few moments, then "Well, Mr. Westbrook, I...."

"Michael. Please call me Michael. I'm not going to bite you!"

"..I really can't say right now, could we just leave it for a week or so?"

"Okay, if that's the best you can do for now, that will have to do. I'll talk to Burns about it when he gets back from holiday. Now, let's get back to work. Would you bring me the Anderson file?"

Sharon hurried out to the file room, and on handing him the retrieved file asked "Do you want me to come back with my notebook?"

"Yes, please. It'll be faster for me than dictating into this fool machine that Burns got me."

Over the next few days, Sharon grew more and more at ease in his office, occasionally seeing signs of gentleness and vulnerability behind the cool exterior. Sitting in her usual chair behind his closed door, pencil poised over her steno book waiting for the next rush of dictation, she watched him pacing back and forth beside his desk, dictating while his fingers ran through the thick hair at his temples, or sitting up with his elbows on his desk, his hand shading his eyes as he pondered the file laying open in front of him.

She found herself smiling more and more often, as she took hidden moments to watch him. One morning as he was standing at Sharon's desk the jarring call buzzer sounded above them. They looked up to see that Dennis Fisher's call light had blinked on. Fisher's assistant, Betty, with her purse on her knee as if to go for her coffee break, jumped up and jammed her cigarette into the ashtray on her desk. She picked up her notebook and stomped past Sharon's desk with such fury that several papers blew off the corner of Sharon's desk onto the floor.

Michael bent down murmuring to Sharon, "Here, let me get those. What else does she do, eat rocks for breakfast?" His eyebrows raised as he turned to watch Betty enter Fisher's office and slam the door behind her. His face softened as he turned, smiling at Sharon, and dropped the flighty papers back onto her desk.

Sharon had also discovered that Michael harbored some resentment for the pecking order that existed at Stewart & Company among the partners and lawyers. The discovery was not a surprise to Sharon.

Her assignments in several law offices during the last three summers had opened her eyes to some of the infighting among the lawyers. She had seen senior partners handing many of their bothersome tedious tasks to junior lawyers, or asking a junior member to do all the research and background work then using it to enhance his own reputation without acknowledging the contribution of the junior.

For the second time since Sharon had started work, while she and Michael were behind closed doors working through his pile of files, they were interrupted by William Hird. After only a cursory knock on the door, Hird had reached into Michael's office to throw a file on his desk, saying "This is that fraud case I told you about. The trial is in two months. It's all yours." and shut the door before Michael could respond.

Michael muttered, "Translate that to 'This is a lost cause, I don't want it." as he threw the file onto the credenza behind him.

Sharon had learned, mostly during her after-work commutes with Teri, that Michael had agreed to join the firm if he could become a partner immediately and if his son, David, could do his law-student articling year with Stewart, Hird & Company.

"I think Michael wants to be closer to his son." Teri had mentioned. "He encouraged David to get his law degree, and I wouldn't be surprised if they decide to open their own office someday."

"So you don't think Michael is really committed to Stewart & Company?" asked Sharon.

"Not really. He doesn't show it much, but I think family is all he really cares about now."

"Wow, that's a surprise. I really can't figure that man out at all."

"I'm not sure why his marriage fell apart, but I know that his ex-wife had sole custody of David during his teenage years and she sent him to residential private schools until he had started University. I think Michael was allowed full custody during the summer breaks from school.

"It sounds so cold and unfeeling. I wonder if David has issues too."

"He seems like a good kid. Really likes to play."

Sharon's evening commutes with Teri had been the perfect end for each day. She enjoyed listening to Teri's stories and it made the drive home interesting and almost too short.

CHAPTER 10

A few days later, slightly breathless as she hurried down the hall toward her work station, Sharon was surprised to see all three of the law students at her desk at the far end of the hall, David sitting on the edge of Sharon's desk, facing his companions.

Nearing her work station, Sharon called, "Hi guys, what brings you to this end of the office so early in the morning?"

Jenny, stepping around David's outstretched feet, held out the papers for Sharon to see. "There's another Will for Mrs. Boyle".

"What?! How can that be?" Tossing her purse onto her chair, Sharon took the pages, her eyes wide. "Oh my God. That's never happened before. When did this come in?"

David stood up, "We got it yesterday, and we've already contacted the office that filed the Notice. They didn't know that Mrs. Boyle had died."

Sharon noticed Fisher's secretary, Betty, walking down the hallway toward them. "Here's Betty coming in, let's see what she knows..."

Ravi whispered "Are we allowed to get information from her?"

"It's okay, Ravi, this is different." Ignoring Betty's usual early morning frown, Sharon stepped beside her as she turned toward her desk. "Hi Betty, sorry to bother you so early in the morning, but we've run into a problem with Mary Boyle's Will."

"What's that got to do with me?"

"Well, I remember that you and Mr. Fisher were the two witnesses on her Will, so I presume you prepared it. It was signed about a year ago."

"Is she dead?"

"Yes, about ten days ago. The care home phoned our estate lawyer, and he assigned the file to Michael for the students to work on."

"Oh yeah, I think I remember now. She was that rich old broad who gave everything to a bunch of charities, wasn't she?"

Ravi and David looked at each other, surprise in their eyes, as they moved closer to the conversation.

"It looks like she did another will about a month after the one we did here. Isn't that kind of unusual?"

"Yeah, maybe. I guess Fisher wasn't charming enough for her. She probably had second thoughts about letting our lawyer handle her estate." She paused. "Anyway, it's not the first time."

"What do you mean?," asked Sharon.

"A couple of years ago, when I first started here, Fisher got screwed out of a really big Executor's fee when this old guy died right after he had changed his Will."

"Did anyone check into that will? Was it prepared by a lawyer?"

"Oh yeah, it was a good Will all right. Fisher even knew the lawyer who prepared it."

Sharon sighed and turned to the students, "Okay, gang, we'll need to talk to Mr. Westbrook about this. I'll call you when he comes in and is ready for us."

David and Ravi started down the hall toward their office, but Jenny held back and walked with Sharon into her cubicle by the window. "Sharon, I think we should do a bit of investigating, don't you? What if there is some kind of error in Mrs. Boyle's replacement Will? And why did the care home call this office when she died, and not the lawyer who prepared that new Will?

"I agree, Jenny. Let's see what Westbrook says."

"Okay, see you later," waved Jenny as she turned to follow her office-mates.

Later that afternoon, with Sharon and all three students seated anxiously in front of his desk, Michael took a moment to throw a foolscap notepad onto his desk blotter, rattle around in his top drawer for pens, clear his throat, then lean back in his chair with a grin on his face to look at all four faces. "I hear you have a problem."

David spoke up first, "Dad, we don't think we can probate the Will we have. The search reply we got back from Vital Statistics reports a more recent Will was signed by Mrs. Boyle about a month before she died."

Before Westbrook could speak, Jenny burst forth with "But we think there's something wrong here, because Stewart, Hird & Company was still on record at the care home as the next-of-kin, and we still get all her bank statements and investment reports from her financial adviser. Why didn't she change everything when she changed her Will?"

Michael held up his hand, "Hold on a minute, let's just slow down and work through this, one thing at a time." Looking directly at Sharon, he motioned to her to take notes, then turned to the students, "First of all, did you get a copy of this other Will?

Ravi spoke up, "We phoned the law firm, but they won't release anything until they get proof of Mrs. Boyle's death. We've faxed a copy of the Death Certificate to them, and we're waiting for a copy of the Will."

Sitting forward in his chair, Michael picked up a pen. "Okay, all probate work comes to a halt until we know more about that new Will." Scribbling a quick list as he spoke, he gave his rapt audience details of their next steps, then standing up at his desk to motion their dismissal, he announced, "Now, any outgoing letters you prepare will be signed by me, but any interviews or investigations you undertake are to be under your own names. You all have your own business cards, use them. Any questions?"

Responding to Michael's body language, all three students crowded through the door, leaving Sharon and Michael alone.

Seeing Sharon's raised eyebrows, Michael smiled "What's that look for? I'm not here to make things easy for them."

Early the next morning, Jenny caught up with Sharon as she entered the reception area on the way to her desk. "Hi Sharon, can I ask you a favor?"

"Sure Jenny, follow me to my desk and we can talk. I just need to make sure Westbrook isn't chomping at the bit."

"The boys and I have decided it would be best for you and I to go to the care home where Mrs. Boyle died, to talk to the nursing staff."

"Are you sure? Why not just the three of you?"

"We all thought two females would probably be able to get more information, especially if there are personal details." Jenny chuckled, "Besides, those boys can be pretty intimidating when they get an idea in their heads, and we don't want them scaring anyone."

Sharon smiled, "So Stewart & Company is growing two more insensitive, egotistical lawyers to send out into the world?"

"Well, maybe not quite that bad. I still hope to soften them up a bit before we've finished our articling year."

"Good for you," grinned Sharon, as they reached her desk. "It looks like Westbrook isn't in yet, so we can talk. When and where are we going?"

"I'll need to get back to you on that. We're trying to choose a time when Mrs. Boyle's attending nurse and the head nurse are both available. It's at that beautiful Lansdowne Care Home near the University. Is it okay if it's on a weekend?"

"Sure, I'm flexible. My Aunt is staying at my place for a few months, but we probably won't be that long anyway, will we?"

"No, I don't think so. And I'll make sure you get paid for your time there too."

As Jenny walked back to the student's lair, Sharon grinned, "Here I am, ten years older and a foot taller than her, and she's my boss."

Later that afternoon Sharon answered her phone, "Hi Jenny, what's up?"

"We've set up an appointment at Lansdowne for this Saturday morning. I hope 8:00 a.m. isn't too early. It's right after the nurses have finished their night shifts."

Glancing at her watch, Sharon answered "Well, it's not my favorite time to be out of bed on a Saturday morning, but I'm really curious about this whole thing. I'll meet you there."

CHAPTER 11

The next Saturday morning, Sharon threw herself out of bed as soon as her alarm sounded and put on a comfortable pants suit over her long-sleeved white shirt, the open collar folded over the jacket collar and lapels. She tiptoed into the kitchen and turned on the coffee machine.

Turning back toward her bedroom, she stopped short at seeing Desi standing in the hallway in her long flannel nightgown, sleepily rubbing her eyes. "Oh Desi, I'm so sorry, I didn't want to wake you."

"Don't be silly, I should be up already."

Sharon bent down to kiss Desi's cheek, "The coffee should be ready in a minute. I'm just going to fix my hair and makeup."

After they had shared their breakfast toast and jam, Sharon jumped up, "Must be on my way, Desi. I need to meet Jenny at eight this morning."

"That's okay," yawned Desi. "I'm feeling sleepy this morning, so I'll just sit for a while before I get dressed."

Sharon threw a notebook into her bag as she opened her door. She was expecting to be taking notes as she and Jenny met with the nurses. Closing the door, she held the door handle until she heard the latch click into place, trying to avoid making any noise.

As usual, she was behind on her schedule, and ran to her car as the elevator doors closed behind her. "Darn, I hope the traffic isn't too bad getting over to Lansdowne." she thought. She sat in her car watching through the rear-view mirror with impatience for the garage security gate to come down, drumming her fingers on the steering wheel.

Arriving at the reception area in Lansdowne, breathless after her run from the parking lot, Sharon saw Jenny leaning onto the receptionists counter, apparently having to show her credentials to the man standing behind the receptionist.

"We have an appointment, I spoke to the manager several days ago," Jenny's voice showing her anxiety, the color on her cheeks starting to flame, "Oh, here's my assistant now."

"Yes, I recall the arrangement. The nurses should be finished their shifts in a few minutes. We can have you wait in the family room just down the hall to your right." The manager frowned slightly.

Before leaving the counter, Jenny asked "Will they have Mrs. Boyle's medical history and records to refer to?"

"I'll bring those items into the family room and put them on the table."

Walking one step behind the manager as he turned toward the hallway, Jenny followed him as she motioned to Sharon to follow, saying "Thank you very much. Mr. Schmidt, is it? We really appreciate your cooperation."

"Yes, I'm Marcus Schmidt." He pointed to the family room door as he walked past it. "If you need anything more from me, the receptionist will let me know."

Jenny opened the door to the empty family room and motioned for Sharon to step inside. They moved directly to the small round table in the middle, choosing seats beside each other. Sharon pulled the notebook and several pens from her bag and placed them on the table. Jenny pulled the office file from her briefcase, and opened the folder.

"Do you think they will let us make copies of anything?" Sharon asked.

"I hope so. Mr. Westbrook said we should have no trouble."

After a few minutes Schmidt opened the door and put two large binders on the table near one of the empty chairs. "The nurses are on their way in."

Before Jenny could finish her second "Thank you", two nurses appeared at the door. The larger tall nurse, frowning, stepped through the door ahead of the younger nurse, who glanced at Jenny and Sharon with a nervous smile on her face.

Jenny stood up and held out her hand "Hello, my name is Jenny Carson, I am with the law firm of Stewart & Company." She shook hands with the nervous nurse who stood closest to her and then motioned toward Sharon, saying "And this is my assistant, Sharon. Thank you so much for taking the time."

"You're welcome," said the taller nurse, her frown fading as she allowed a tentative smile to appear on her lips. She reached across the table to shake Jenny's outstretched hand and said, "I'm Trudy Masters, and this is Brenda Brown."

Jenny nodded, saying, "Please have a seat" as she motioned to the two remaining chairs at the table. "Do you mind if I record our conversations? It will help my assistant when she prepares the notes from our visit."

Sharon had already arranged herself in the dictation-receiving position, with her chair set back from the table, her knees crossed, her notebook and pen in her hands, resting on her upper knee. She had already written down the nurses' names after the date and time which always appeared at the top of her first page of notes. She rested against the back of her chair, watching her table-mates for movement to signal that words would follow.

Jenny reached down into her briefcase and placed a small recorder about the size of a deck of cards onto the middle of the table.

Trudy frowned slightly. Glancing at Brenda with a questioning look, she said "No, I'm sure it's quite proper, if you feel a recording is necessary."

Brenda nodded her acceptance.

"Thank you very much." Jenny smiled and turning her eyes away from the tiny red light now glowing from the end of the small device, she leaned forward and looked from Brenda to Trudy, saying, "Now, I understand you were both on duty the night Mrs. Boyle died?"

Trudy answered, "Yes, she was a very good patient and easy to care for. She had been at Lansdowne for over two years."

Lifting up the pages attached to her folder, Jenny said "Yes, I see that. Now, as you know, my law firm had been listed as next-of-kin for Mrs. Boyle, and we were contacted by Lansdowne the morning after her death."

Trudy answered, "Yes, I remember that."

"We had also prepared Mrs. Boyle's Will, and were expecting to be handling her estate, but we have since learned that she apparently prepared another Will a few weeks prior to her death. We need to have more information about that Will and hope to find out why Mrs. Boyle did not inform us of her changed plans."

Trudy huffed, then said "Well, we don't know anything about the legal stuff, but we've got all Mrs. Boyle's records here. What do you need to know?"

"Was Mrs. Boyle in the habit of leaving your facility?"

Brenda spoke up, "Mrs. Boyle was such a sweet little thing. We had lots of interesting talks on her good days, and there was a friend of hers that sometimes took her out in a wheelchair for outings. She was very frail, but really enjoyed getting out. They even went out to an afternoon movie a couple of weeks before she died."

"Did you keep notes of the times she was away?"

"Of course. This is a very secure facility. We keep complete records of our patients," Trudy frowned as she shifted impatiently to open the binder marked "Mary Boyle".

Sharon whispered to Jenny, "Could we get copies of Mrs. Boyle's records?"

Jenny nodded, and was about to ask for the copies, when Brenda smiled and sighed, apparently recollecting something. Jenny turned to Brenda and asked in a quiet voice, "Did you and Mrs. Boyle become friends?"

Tears appeared in Brenda's eyes, "I like to think so. She loved telling me about her life and all the travels she and her husband had taken. They never had children and she would touch my hand and tell me I was like a daughter to her. And she especially loved it when I brushed her long white hair and put it into braids for her. I really miss her."

"It sounds as though you remember a lot about her?" asked Jenny.

"And she was funny too, always ready to laugh at herself when she was embarrassed."

"Please, feel free to tell us anything you think might be of interest."

Brenda's smile broke as she continued with her recollections, "I remember Mrs. Boyle laughing about that trip to see the movie with her friend. She joked about spending money to buy a ticket to sleep."

Trudy interrupted before Brenda could continue, "Brenda, I'm sure these people don't need all this idle chit chat about Mrs. Boyle. Just let them ask their questions."

Jenny interjected, "We are interested in any information you can provide, please don't worry about wasting our time. We're sorry to be holding you back from leaving, but if we could get a copy of your daily reports on Mrs. Boyle that would show when she was absent, and if possible when she had visitors."

"The only visitor she ever had was that lady who was a volunteer from some agency. They became friends and she was the only person who took Mrs. Boyle on outings. We have her name and signature on the schedules from each time they went out together. I always put in little notes about what Mrs. Boyle told me, so that I could help her remember and talk about her outings. She loved to tell me stories about things she had done in her lifetime."

A short while later, with Brenda still happily chattering away about her memories of Mrs. Boyle, Trudy slammed open the binder, pulled out all the pages in it and stood up, "I'll just take these to the office for copying. I'll just be a minute while Brenda finishes her stories." On her return, Trudy dropped the copies in front of Jenny and remained standing as if to dismiss the meeting, although Sharon was still scribbling shorthand notes in her book.

Jenny turned to Sharon, "Are your notes okay? Do you have any questions?"

Sharon looked up as she finished her last scribble, "No, I'm done. The recorder will fill in my blanks."

Jenny smiled, stood up and held out her hand to Trudy, "Thank you very much for your assistance, we really appreciate the information you've provided."

Trudy's face looking stern, she shook Jenny's hand and walked toward the open door as Brenda offered her hand to Jenny, smiling, "Oh thank you, it's been very special for me to think about sweet little Mrs. Boyle again. I really became very attached to her."

Outside in the parking lot, Sharon, holding the copied pages, touched Jenny's arm in alarm as she pointed to an entry, "Look, Jenny, the day Mrs. Boyle was out at the movies is the same date as that new Will! Brenda didn't say anything about Mrs. Boyle doing a Will on that day."

CHAPTER 12

The next Monday morning, as Sharon sat ready to take dictation from Michael, he asked "So, how did the visit to Lansdowne go on Saturday?"

Sharon straightened up, eyebrows raised in surprise "Oh, I didn't know you knew.."

"David keeps me up to date on all their shenanigans. I'm the articling students' mentor, after all. So, what do you think?"

"I think there's something strange going on." Sharon paused, glancing at Michael, "That new Will was dated the same day that Mrs. Boyle was out with a friend. I think we should get more details about those circumstances."

"You and Jenny are probably over-reacting. People change their Wills all the time."

Feeling defensive, Sharon said, "Well, Mrs. Boyle was very frail and wheelchair-bound. I don't know, something just doesn't feel right to me.

"Okay, you and the students can continue investigating for now, although I'm not certain female intuition should be coming into the equation. Anyway, we do need to at least see and touch the original of that other Will and compare it to the copy that was faxed to us. After that we'll go over what you learned from the hospital before we make any decision."

"Thank you, I'll tell Jenny we have your approval for now."

"David told me he's planning to see the lawyer who prepared that new Will. I want you to go with David and Ravi when they meet that lawyer. That way you can report everything to me as well as Jenny so that all the students know what's going on. I've already spoken to the lawyer, he's an old buddy of mine, and he's agreed to cooperate."

A few days later, Sharon and Ravi piled into David's convertible, Sharon riding in the front passenger seat at David's request, for their trip to the uptown district where the lawyer's office was located.

Sharon couldn't help but look over at David as the three of them carried on their conversation. Sharon had turned in her seat so that she and Ravi could hear each other above the wind whipping around them as they drove.

She noticed that David had almost the same profile as his father, but his lips were fuller and his hair was darker and cut short. His white shirt collar showing above his light gray sport jacket brought out the contrast to his healthy-looking tan. His posture was almost military, with his chin tucked into his long, straight neck and his shoulders pushed back, his right arm held straight out to the top of the steering wheel.

He glanced at Sharon, a mischievous grin on his face as he sped past slower vehicles, took corners almost on two wheels and slammed on the brakes just before each red light.

Sharon stopped trying to have a conversation. She turned to face the windshield and braced herself, one hand on the door, her other on her seat belt buckle.

They pulled into a metered parking space in front of a long two-storey building. The ground floor contained full-windowed business offices. The top floor was all apartments, with balcony railings adorned with planters overflowing with flowers and greenery. Except for this commercial block, the surrounding area was all residential, filled with tree-lined avenues bordered by well-kept lawns and flower gardens leading to elegant older homes.

There was very little foot traffic, and few vehicles to disturb the peace of the morning. The area became all the more quiet as soon as David had shut down the engine of his sports car.

"Well, thank you David, that was an exciting trip. Can I put my stomach back down where it belongs?" Sharon remarked as she struggled out of the low-slung front seat. Ravi stood up behind her seat and vaulted himself over the side of the car onto the sidewalk.

"That's nothing, wait until I get you out on my sailboat" boasted David. "You're not afraid of sailing too, are you?"

"I'm not afraid of riding in a car either, if the driver isn't insane," laughed Sharon.

David opened the glass door to the office, leaning against the gilded words "Charles Everson, Barrister and Solicitor" . He motioned Sharon and Ravi to enter the small office while he held the door. Inside, he stepped ahead of them to announce their appointment and continued to stand at the front counter as though not willing to sit down and wait.

Soon afterward all three of them were shown into a small conference room next to the reception area, where a disheveled-looking, overweight middle-aged man was sitting at the end of the oval table, leafing through the file before him. He stood up, extended his hand to David, "I'm Charles Everson" then to Ravi and Sharon, "I'm not sure what you hope to find."

David motioned for Ravi and Sharon to take the seats across the table from him. "We were surprised to find that our client had made another Will after the one our firm had prepared for her. We felt that our due diligence required at least a look into the circumstances of the Will you prepared. We appreciate your co-operation."

Everson raised his eyebrows slightly, "Well, it seemed pretty straightforward to me, nothing unusual, I mean. You did receive the copy I sent you?"

"Yes, the copy came through clearly enough. I have it here in our file." David pulled out three pages, stapled, and set them down in front of Everson.

"We just need to see the original for comparison."

Everson laughed, "Sounds like you've already experienced the Probate Registrar's nosy questions about staples being removed and the color of ink used for signatures."

David glanced at Sharon, his eyebrows raised. "Can't be too careful about these things, especially with the size of Mrs. Boyle's estate." Sharon nodded as she smiled at him.

Everson opened his file and slid it towards David so that they could both see the contents. After a moment, he stated, "I just took brief notes about her assets when I talked to her on the phone before we made an appointment. We didn't go into too much detail about the actual value, because she was talking to me from her care home location."

"I see", said David. "Do you mind if we have a quick look at your file?"

"Certainly not, help yourself. I'll get the original Will out of our vault in the meantime." Everson pushed the file closer to David and left the door open as he turned to walk toward the back of his office.

David looked up, "Sharon, come sit beside me here and have a look at this. Let me know if you have any questions."

As Sharon sat down, Ravi whispered "What's this about staples and colors?"

Sharon glanced toward the open door then in a hushed voice directed at both Ravi and David, "The Registrar asks questions if the signatures of the testator and both witnesses are not all done with the same pen or at least the same color of pen."

"Why?", asked Ravi.

"Because all three people are supposed to be together watching each other sign and initial the Will at the same time, like the words say on the last page of the Will."

Ravi was about to ask another question when Everson entered the room and shut the door, muttering, "Well, it seems that we might have slipped up on something here."

He sat down and unfolded the document in his one hand. His other hand held a white envelope embossed with the word "Will" in a large Old English printing style.

All eyes were on Everson. David cleared his throat, "Is there a problem?"

Everson frowned. "I don't know how this happened, but the original Will has been removed from the Will envelope. This is just a photocopy, identical to the one in my file and the one I sent to your office."

Sharon, feeling protective of the inexperience of David and Ravi, moved forward in her chair and asked, "Do you have any information about where the original Will is now?" The sudden silence hit her and she immediately sat back behind David, feeling embarrassed at speaking up.

Everson sat back in his chair, a quizzical look on his face as he looked back and forth between Sharon and David.

David spoke directly to Everson, "Sharon's been a legal assistant for a thousand years and she's almost finished at law school, so she's a valuable commodity in our office."

Everson grinned at the three of them, "Well, she's asked a good question. There is a note in this envelope saying that the original Will was released to the Executor named in the Will. Let's see, that seems to be a person by the name of Lizzy Placer."

Encouraged by Everson's remark, Sharon looked over David's shoulder at the open file and asked, "Is there a copy of Mrs. Boyle's identification documents in the file?"

"No, I never keep those copies in the file."

Eyebrows raised, David looked up at Everson, "I'm sorry?"

"But I do take ID. I never witness anyone's signature unless I've seen their ID first. My girls scan the ID into a special folder in our computer system."

"So you are able to print out a copy of that ID?" David asked.

"Well, yes, but I usually just pull it up on my computer screen to look at when the client is in front of me, ready to sign."

"Would you mind giving us a copy?"

"Sure," as he picked up the phone and pushed the intercom button, "Hi sweetie, could you print me a copy of the ID for Mary Boyle?"

Looking relieved, David turned to continue leafing through Everson's file, "Do you recall anything unusual about Mrs. Boyle?

"No, not really. She seemed fairly frail, and obviously needed her walker for support when she came into this room, but she was alert and friendly."

"Did she have any questions about her Will after she had read it?"

"No, she seemed to scan through it quickly and was anxious to get it over with."

"Were you able to get more details about her estate?"

"Well, she finally blurted out something about being worth over a million and that all the information would be with her other papers in her safety deposit box."

The office receptionist opened the door and dropped two sheets of paper in front of Everson. David turned to her, "Thank you." as he leaned over to look at the sheets.

Everson pushed the papers toward David, "She had a government picture ID card instead of a driver's license and she also had her health care card."

Holding the sheets up so that all three of them could see, David asked Everson, "Do you think this picture ID was a good likeness of her?"

"Well, she kind of chuckled about that, saying that she had been ill about four years ago when the picture was taken, and had put on a bit of weight since then."

"But her hair and facial features did match this picture otherwise?"

"Here, let me look at that again," said Everson as he reached for the copy of the government picture ID. "Oh yes, I remember now, because I thought it unusual to see white hair in braids. She had her hair up in braids, just like that picture."

"Okay, did she have any trouble signing?" David took the paper from Everson and laid it down beside the last page of the Will. "The signature on her Will looks quite different than the one on her ID..."

"Yes, I agree. As I said, like a lot of elderly people, her hand went all shaky when she picked up the pen to sign."

"Sharon, what do you think? I know you've probably witnessed a lot of Wills over the years?"

Surprised at his request, Sharon looked up at David, "Yes, I agree. People are often very nervous just being in front of a lawyer. Maybe we should just take copies of everything in his file, including his notes, to go over when we get back to our office?"

David turned with a slight shrug to Everson, hopefulness showing in his smile and raised eyebrows, "Would you mind, Mr. Everson?"

"No, not at all, I'd rather just co-operate now than go through all the Court garbage if there's a problem." Everson picked up his file and opened the door, calling "Hey Jessie, would you be a dear and make copies of everything in this file?"

Seeing the file leaving the room, Sharon spoke up, "Is there a note in there about when you first met with Mrs. Boyle to obtain her instructions for her Will?"

Everson turned back into the room. "Oh yes, I remember now. When we talked on the phone, she asked if I could come to the Lansdowne Care Home to talk about changing her Will. She told me she just wanted a very simple Will, but when I told her I would need her doctor's letter of competency first if she wanted me to see her at her care home, she asked if she could just tell me her wishes over the phone. She sounded pretty frail and didn't want to make an extra trip if she could avoid it. Most of my notes were made from our phone conversations."

David took the lead again, "So you didn't actually meet with her before she arrived to sign her Will?"

"No, but I had a couple of conversations with her over the phone when I asked her for more details of her assets and family. It's not often you run into an only child with both parents being only children. I remember her being slightly annoyed at some of my questions, but she did call me back several times with the information."

"Did she say why she wanted to do a new Will?"

"Apparently her old Will gave everything to charity, and she had decided to help out a few of her friends instead."

David lifted up his copy of the Will, and pointed to the middle of the second page, "So this Marion Mason named as one of the beneficiaries in the Will is one of those friends?"

"Yes, she told me they had been inseparable as children."

"This other beneficiary, Brenda Brown, is described as her dedicated caregiver. Did she give you details?"

The door opened and Everson reached back to take the file and copies from his assistant, saying, "No, but I think she was one of the nurses at the care home."

"Did Mrs. Boyle come by herself to sign her Will, or was someone with her?"

"Hold on there, young fellow. Let me look at my notes again. I want to be sure."

After a few moments of silence, David put his hand on the copies that Everson had pushed across the table. "I'm sorry, Mr. Everson. We shouldn't be using any more of your time. Perhaps we could telephone you after we have had a chance to study your file?"

"No bother, I enjoy meeting enthusiastic young people. Let me see, yes, her friend from childhood was Marion Mason, and yes, she came alone to my office."

"And you said that she didn't have a wheelchair?"

"Not that I remember, I'm sure it was just a walker. She looked quite frail and weak, but her mind was sharp as a tack."

After a short lull in their closing chitchat, David tapped his fingers on the table and motioned toward the door for Ravi and Sharon. They all stood up and David extended his hand to Everson, "Thank you very much, sir, we really appreciate your assistance."

As they walked to the car, Sharon whispered to David and Ravi, "Brenda Brown is the name of the nurse that Jenny and I saw on Saturday at the care home."

CHAPTER 13

Sharon knew that the three students would need some time to consider the Mary Boyle file and all the additional information they had gathered since discovering the existence of the second Will. She had typed out all the notes she had made from her and Jenny's visit to the hospital. She had also delivered to Jenny for her approval the report prepared from Jenny's notes summarizing all the other phone calls and inquiries Jenny had completed on her own.

David and Ravi had also handed to Sharon their notes made after their visit to Everson and a review of Everson's file. Sharon was enjoying copying from David's notes. She liked his handwriting, she thought it had an easy flair, an unhurried slant, the look of a small sailboat under the full sail of a soft summer wind. Her eyes must have taken on a faraway, dreamy look, as she sat at her computer.

With her unthinking fingers flying over the keyboard, she transcribed the graceful lines into digital data, soon to be spit onto paper in triplicate.

"Hey, Sharon girl, where are you?" chuckled Anna, as she looked at Sharon while turning toward her own desk from the hallway.

Sharon leaned in her chair to see around her computer, "Oh darn, now I'm awake again" she laughed at Anna. "Good thing my fingers kept working, eh?"

"You're busted my friend. I saw that look in your eyes," Anna grinned as she pushed her reading glasses back into place. "I'll have a talk with you at coffee, you can count on that."

Sharon gave her head a shake, took a deep breath, bent toward the papers on her desk, then looked up at the computer monitor. Pleased to see that she had almost finished the last of David's notes, she sharpened her focus and willed her eyes and fingers into high gear.

Sharon kept up her frantic pace so completely that she didn't notice Westbrook standing at his door, looking around the corner at her. He cleared his throat, causing Sharon to jump in her chair and lift her hands off the keyboard.

Looking up, able to see only his left shoulder and head leaning out from his door, like a squirrel peeking from around a tree, she let out an involuntary laugh. "I'm sorry, did you need me? I didn't hear my buzzer go." She couldn't wipe the grin from her face, nor get the twinkle out of her eyes.

"No", smiled Westbrook, "I just heard a slight commotion out here."

"I'm almost finished the students' notes now," Sharon interrupted, not giving Westbrook any chance to complain. She wondered if his appearance was his attempt to control office chit chat, and felt slight annoyance at that thought.

Michael nodded, "That's good. David wants to arrange a meeting for all of us to discuss the Mary Boyle file. Can we set it for tomorrow afternoon?"

"Whatever your schedule allows." Sharon smiled up at him, "I'll finish printing out their notes today, so they'll have time to review them before the meeting."

Sharon turned back to the papers in front of her, shutting out any further interruption and letting her automatic pilot take over hands, fingers and thought. Just before the end of the day she stood up and stretched as her printer spit out the last page of the students' notes.

On her way out to meet Teri for the drive home, she popped into the students' hideaway and dropped three copies onto the table. All three students had large tomes opened on the table before them and hardly looked up as Sharon backed out and closed the door.

CHAPTER 14

Late in the afternoon on the next day, Sharon had finished most of her work. She relaxed for a moment at her desk and checked her watch. The appointed hour for the students' meeting with Westbrook had arrived. As she watched the three students walking up the hall toward her, she picked up her phone and pushed the intercom button.

With all three students now gathered around Sharon's desk, she looked up as she waited for Westbrook to answer the intercom. Letting her eyes wander to their faces, she smiled as she noticed their anxious looks, thinking "They all look like baby birds waiting for mommy to drop the worm."

Westbrook's voice broke into her reverie and she leaned in over her notebook, pencil ready to scribble, saying, "Hi, the students are here now. Shall we all come in?" She smiled up at them again, "Okay, we will," and replaced the phone into its cradle. Turning to David, she said "He wants us to bring my chair in."

David smiled, then saluted and stepped behind Sharon, saying "At your command, my lady."

"Thank you, Good Sir" she laughed as she stood up and picked up her notebook and pencils.

Jenny stepped first to Westbrook's door and opened it, hesitating as she looked in, then trotted to the chair next to the window. Sitting down, she nodded toward Westbrook, "Thank you, sir"

Ravi and David followed her, David grinning as he rolled Sharon's chair into place behind Jenny. "Three Musketeers, reporting in, sir."

Michael smiled, "Sure, and I'm the King of France." Leaning back in his chair, he said, "So, what's the story?"

Jenny and Ravi both turned to David, as he lifted their papers and dropped them on the corner of the desk, "Well, Dad, we brought the file and all our notes, but you've probably already seen our notes from Sharon."

Michael sat forward in his chair, pulling forward the front edges of his jacket before he stretched out his arms ahead of him. "I just took a quick glance at them to see how long we might need. I'd like to hear it from all of you for now, I'll read the stuff later."

Ravi and David relaxed back in their chairs, turning to Jenny. She took her cue, and with a slight frown announced, "The bottom line is, Mrs. Boyle's last Will seems at first glance to be valid, but there are too many odd circumstances around it, in my opinion."

Michael smiled at Jenny's words then raised his eyebrows as he looked directly at Sharon, "That female intuition again?"

David looked startled as he sat forward, "No, Dad, the girls are right. Look at the list we made."

Michael picked up the sheets and sat back in his chair. "Okay, she didn't tell anyone she had made a new Will, the nurses hadn't seen her use a walker for over a year, her signature doesn't match her ID, healthier looking than her ID picture...hmm." He sat reading through the list, all eyes watching him in expectation.

As Michael lifted his eyes from the list, Ravi remarked in his quiet voice, "We think it bears further investigation, Mr. Westbrook."

"That may be so," smiled Michael, "but who is going to pay for an investigation? The only people who might benefit would be the two charities that Mrs. Boyle asked us to name as her sole beneficiaries in that first Will. And the charities would only benefit if the second Will was proven to be invalid."

Jenny pulled her fingers across her forehead, lifting her hair away from her eyes, "It could also mean a big embarrassment for this Everson lawyer, if a Court hearing proved that he had been lacking in due diligence. His notes seemed a bit sketchy about her circumstances."

"Everson is an old buddy of mine." Michael's tone was almost defensive, "He's been around long enough to know what's important with Wills. He would have found out if there had been any sign of undue influence on Mrs. Boyle, and he would certainly have checked for mental competence. That's a given, regardless of what his notes say."

David had been sitting in silence, and sat up slightly at the temporary lull. "So, it's not really up to us to do anything about this new Will. Should we just close our file and let Everson's Will go through Probate?"

Michael sat rubbing his chin for a moment, his other hand still holding the list. "I'll tell you what, people. Get me the names of the law firms that those two charities use for Probate matters, and I'll give them a call. We'll let them advise their clients and find out whether or not the charities want to take a gamble and try to challenge Everson's Will."

"That could run into a lot of money for the charities," David remarked.

Michael dropped the list onto his desk, "Well, Mrs. Boyle's estate is worth well over fifteen million from what I can see. And there's a possibility that the lawyers will take the case on a contingency basis if they think there is enough evidence to invalidate that second Will."

He rolled his chair back from his desk and looked toward the door, before looking again at the students.

David nodded and motioned to Ravi to move, as he stood up, "Thanks Dad. We've got some ideas on more questions that need answers, and maybe those law firms will agree. We'll get their numbers to you right away."

Michael nodded as he pulled the students' file toward him, "I'll be reviewing this stuff in the meantime." He stood up and asked "By the way, I'd like individual written opinions from each of you on whether you would challenge the Will if it was up to you and if you would do it on a contingency basis. I want you to consider your position as if you were business owners, responsible for your own staff and overhead costs." Michael grinned at them and waved them toward the door.

David and Ravi stumbled over each other's feet as they hurried to move their chairs and get out. As she was turning to follow them, Jenny turned to Michael, "Thank you again, Mr. Westbrook." She smiled as she reached out toward the door, "Do you want your door left open?"

"Sure, that's fine," Michael waved at Jenny, then turning to Sharon he asked "Have you got a few minutes?"

Sharon, standing beside her chair ready to roll it out to her desk, straightened up with surprise, "Oh, okay. No problem." and sat down.

Michael took a breath, gathered up all the papers in front of him and stuffed them into the file folder. "Would you mind organizing this file for me? If there isn't already a short list, I'd like you to prepare a sheet setting out the main concerns. When you have it ready, I'll call the other lawyers."

"David's summary was pretty complete, but I can make sure nothing gets missed."

He shoved the stuffed folder across the desk and leaned toward Sharon, "So, just give me a quick heads up. What do you think about this Boyle matter?"

Sharon reached over to pick up the folder, then turned as she put it onto her chair. Not certain whether Michael was actually interested in her opinion, she quipped, "Well, I think either Mrs. Boyle just got a bee in her bonnet to change her Will and didn't want her favorite nurse to find out about it, or somebody has figured out a way to gather enough information and ID to impersonate an old lady."

"So how would you do it?" Michael smiled.

Sharon looked at him with a quizzical frown, "How would I do what?"

"Prove one way or the other." Michael seemed to be enjoying the banter, as he strolled around his desk toward the door.

Her arms feeling shaky, Sharon had grasped her chair and was starting to roll it toward the door. She stopped suddenly, realizing that he was standing in her path and apparently waiting for her answer. "Well, I'd find out more about everybody."

"Like who?"

She looked up at Michael, wondering what was going on behind that grin.

Taking a deep breath, she said "Well, the nurse, and the friend who took Mrs. Boyle on outings in her wheelchair. And probably the Executor and the other beneficiary named in the Will. And anyone who saw Mrs. Boyle on the day the Will was signed, stuff like that."

Michael moved next to Sharon and pulled her chair away from her hands, "Here, let me roll this thing out." He leaned forward and chuckled as he rolled Sharon's chair away from her, out through his door and back to her desk.

Sharon followed him, no further words coming from her. He stood up, turning to look at Sharon, "That relaxed, calm look of yours sure hides a wild imagination."

Sharon could feel her cheeks warming, her tongue tied up with frustration, thinking "There's nothing wrong with my imagination." She couldn't look at him as he passed in front of her.

Turning toward his office door, he glanced down the hallway and muttered "Looks like the lemmings have already deserted the land."

Sharon wanted to remind him that it was after five o'clock, but her teeth were still clenched. Noticing that the three other legal assistants in her work area had already abandoned their desks, Sharon picked up the folder from her chair and threw it in the cupboard above her desk. Bending down to yank her purse out from it's hiding place on the floor, she turned to stomp down the hallway toward her escape.

Sharon could feel Michael's eyes watching her until she had turned to enter the waiting room. She was certain that he was standing at his door with a grin on his face.

"Whoa Nellie!" yelled Teri, as she stepped back at Sharon's headlong entrance into the waiting room. "You look like a bull ready to charge." Teri laughed, "I was just going to come looking for you."

"I'm sorry, Teri," gasped Sharon, stopping short to catch her breath, "I hope I'm not holding you up."

"No, not at all, just calm down." Teri reached out to touch Sharon's arm. "Anyway, you know the later we are, the better the traffic gets."

"Okay, just let me grab my coat. I can't get away from him fast enough," muttered Sharon as she trotted out into the elevator lobby.

"Take it easy, girl," yelled Teri, "I'm not in a hurry."

Later, while Teri maneuvered her car out of the parking garage and into traffic, Sharon settled into her seat, leaned back onto the headrest and let a sigh escape, listening to the heavy rain pounding on the roof.

Teri glanced over with a playful exaggerated look of concern on her face, then patted Sharon's arm. "Okay, kid, tell me all about it."

"I can't stand him, he drives me crazy," wailed Sharon, sitting forward, "He treats me like I'm an idiot, and it feels like he's always laughing at me."

Teri nodded, "Maybe he's just testing you."

"Well if he's testing to see if I'll quit my job, he's got a long wait ahead of him."

"Good girl," grinned Teri, "That's the spirit I like to see."

"Honestly, I could have spit at him tonight. It makes me so mad when I can't think of a nasty retort to throw back at him, something to get him off his high horse." Sharon unclenched her fists and shut her eyes, resting back against the seat.

For several minutes, as the car coasted slowly along the crowded, wet streets, Sharon let the rhythm of the beating windshield wipers calm her anger.

Taking a quick look toward Sharon's relaxed hands, Teri asked in a quiet voice, "Has he been asking you any more nosy personal questions?"

Sharon stirred in her seat, "What, oh, sorry Teri, I was lost in space there for a second." Sharon rubbed her face with both hands and answered, "No, not lately. He knows I'm single and that I'm taking courses at the university, that's about it."

Teri leaned toward Sharon, "Well, I think he's been digging around for more information. He even asked me something the other day."

Sharon turned to Teri, surprise in her voice, "He did?"

"Yes. He knows that you ride home with me. He asked me if you were dating yet, and mentioned something about what year your husband died."

"Oh God, I can't stand this. Why would he want to know? He's at least twenty-five years older than me and I work for him."

"Well, he does have an eligible son who is just as gorgeous as his dad."

"Oh." Sharon was speechless for a moment, then she turned to Teri, "Okay, Teri. What have you heard?"

Teri laughed. "I haven't heard anything." She glanced at Sharon, "What do you think of David?"

Sharon giggled and rapped her knuckles against Teri's arm, "Oh, I know your tricks, Teri. You'll get me talking about David, and the next thing you know there'll be a rumor flying through the office grapevine about our pending marriage."

"Not from me, there won't." Teri lowered her voice to imitate a masculine tone, and announced, "I stick to hard facts, ma'am, nothing but the facts." She grinned, "So, do you have any facts for me?"

Sharon watched the road ahead, wondering if she had ever thought anything about David, let alone have feelings about him. "I've been so wrapped up with the work and how to deal with Michael, I guess David hasn't even entered my mind."

"Okay, I'll let you off the hook for now."

Another five or six miles passed in idle chit chat about the traffic and the weather, with a few yawns shared between them. Finally Teri slowed down and pulled to the curb, "Okay, Sharon, here's your apartment. Don't forget your umbrella."

"Thank you again, Teri. See you tomorrow." Sharon ran toward the building's main entrance, holding her bag above her to keep the rain off her head, while she splashed through the puddles on the sidewalk, soaking her new navy pumps.

CHAPTER 15

The days turned into weeks, the October days of left-over summer warmth gradually clouded and cooled, becoming the November dreary dark days of unrelenting rain. Sharon and Teri continued their after-work commute in Teri's battered little compact car, Sharon usually thankful to reach her apartment in one piece. Her mind filled with the latest office gossip would provide the entertainment for her and Desi to chuckle over at dinnertime.

Desi's happy smile, her hands rubbing down on her oversized long white apron, greeted Sharon almost every workday. Sharon could feel a contentment growing inside her, a willingness to settle into a future of quiet restful evenings, and weekends spent with Desi, both of then enjoying visits to local tourist destinations, live theater, symphonies and every romantic comedy that was scheduled to show in nearby cinemas.

By mid-November, Desi had learned enough about Sharon's office circumstances and co-workers to know who all the players were and what had been happening in their lives. Sharon had grown accustomed to the routine after her arrival home: throw her purse onto the bench seat in the entrance hallway, hang up her coat, put her dripping umbrella in the wrought-iron holder inside the door and kick off her wet shoes. She and Desi would share a warm hug with Desi's greeting, "Hello, my dear. Did you have a good day?"

Sharon had developed a daily habit, for Desi's benefit, of choosing at least one story to tell at the end of her workdays. Usually it was minor gossip items about the inhabitants of the office, or the description of an unusually exotic-looking new client passing by Sharon's desk. Often it was Sharon's chance to complain about how rude or annoying Michael had been that day. And on uneventful days, it was sometimes only a simple description of an especially delightful flavor of doughnut that had been available that morning in the coffee room.

"We've got some interesting news for today," Sharon announced, her hands on Desi's shoulders.

Desi clapped her palms together, "Oh goodie, I can hardly wait." She spun around toward the kitchen door, "Just let me get our dinners on the table first."

Sharon smiled happily, savoring the aroma as Desi opened the oven door, "It sure smells good. What can I do to help?"

"You just sit down and be a good girl. You've been working hard all day, and I have everything ready for us."

"Wine, too? You'll really loosen my tongue tonight." Sharon grinned as she poured wine into the two goblets.

"You deserve to be treated like a princess, so I made my special chicken cordon-bleu for you, and today's Friday, so you have the whole weekend to relax. So let's say our prayer and then you can tell me all about your day."

Desi bowed her head and recited a very short poem of grace, then lifted her smiling blue eyes to Sharon's, expectancy written all over her face.

"First of all," said Sharon as she lifted her glass of wine toward Desi and waited for her to follow suit, "Cheers."

"Cheers," giggled Desi before they both took sips, then Desi moved her glass toward her chest, and leaned wide-eyed toward Sharon, "Now tell me everything."

"Well, the biggest news is that the charities named in Mrs. B's Will have told their lawyers to put a temporary barrier against that new Will, until they have made further investigations."

"What kind of barrier, how do they do that?"

"I think it's called a Caveat, and it's a paper given to the Court telling them not to grant Probate of the new Will until the lawyers cancel the Caveat."

Sharon had learned over the weeks that Desi was very interested in everything Sharon could tell her, whether it was about Sharon, her workmates, clients or technical legal matters. Knowing that she couldn't divulge information about particular clients or matters covered by privacy laws, Sharon had used nicknames or code names for people and files when she was telling her stories to Desi.

Desi's ability to remember and desire to learn amazed Sharon, and each time Sharon had to do some extra research to answer one of Desi's questions, she realized that she was learning, right along with Desi. They had sometimes filled entire evenings talking and researching information on Sharon's computer. Sharon found that Desi's enthusiasm was contagious.

"So what happens now?" asked Desi.

"Well, it's funny you should ask, because I didn't think we would need to do much, but the charities' lawyers want to talk to me and the three students, and they've already had a long phone conversation with Fisher."

"That sounds exciting, will you need to go to Court?"

"No, I don't think so, but they might want us to swear Affidavits. One thing I know, Betty is madder than a wet hen, because Fisher made her go digging through some old closed files to find an estate file he had been working on when Betty first started working for him a few years back."

Desi laughed, "I'd sure like to meet this Betty, it sounds like she's kind of cranky."

"You did meet her, Desi. She was the other witness when you signed your Will in Fisher's office."

"Oh, her. She seemed fine to me. She smiled and I noticed her hand was very gentle when she took the pen out of my hand to put her initials on my Will. The only negative thing I remember was the smell of cigarettes on her."

"Well, anyway, it was apparently after that old estate file was closed that Fisher started the office policy of taking current photographs of clients who were signing a Will or a Power of Attorney document."

"So it sounds like proof of identification might be really important?

"Yes, partly. To find out if its possible that it wasn't really Mrs. B who signed that new Will. Then if it seems that she did sign the new Will, they'll need to make sure she knew what she was doing and that she wasn't being forced to sign that new Will."

"So that poor old lawyer, Mr. E, is going to be dragged into this too, isn't he?"

"Yes, because he prepared that Will. And probably the people named in the new Will too, especially the nurse because she is a beneficiary of Mrs. B's estate, and she is the last one who saw Mrs. B alive."

"My, my. I wonder if Mrs. B is looking down from Heaven, watching all these goings-on."

"Well, at least from up there she knows the truth. I'm sure it will all work out for the best, one way or the other."

"Yes, I agree my dear, sighed Desi. "I'm so glad to hear you say that, it makes me think about my precious Donald being up there too, watching over us."

CHAPTER 16

One Saturday morning a few weeks before Christmas, Desi and Sharon sat at her little kitchen table, chatting over the last sips of their coffee. Sharon was enjoying the leisurely start to her morning, but Desi was already dressed in her favorite soft blue wool pantsuit. Desi put down her coffee mug and leaned toward Sharon with a daring gleam in her eyes. "Let's go downtown to see Santa Clause and then have lunch at my favorite French restaurant, what do you think?"

Sharon teased Desi, laughing, "I know what you're after. Another kiss from Pierre!"

"I'm guilty. I admit it." chuckled Desi, "But wouldn't it be fun? We can get our picture taken with Santa Clause so I can take it with me back home in January."

Almost startled to hear Desi mention leaving for the Island, Sharon swallowed the lump that pressed her throat. "Oh my goodness, I can't believe how quickly time has gone."

Desi's blue eyes twinkled, "Now, don't you be sad. What's that saying, 'Time Flies When You're Having Fun'?"

"I'm sorry, my sweetie. It's been so nice having you here.."

"And I've been having the time of my life! But I must let you get on with yours. You don't want to be tied to your silly old Aunt for the rest of your life."

"I could live this way forever." Seeing that Desi was determined to go, Sharon sighed, "Okay then let's go have more fun, just let me change into something more picture-worthy."

Desi followed Sharon toward her bedroom, "I think it would be fun to take the bus, so you can relax with me instead of driving."

"Are you sure? I don't mind driving."

"Well if the bus is too awful, I'll pay for a taxi to bring us home. I want us to both have fun."

"Oh Desi, you're such a sweetheart." Sharon pulled her lilac angora sweater over her head, and checked her reflection as she yanked her sweater down over her light gray pants. "With all the Christmas shoppers, there's probably no parking left anyway."

They walked to the bus stop, Sharon glad that the weatherman had co-operated by giving them a bright cloud-free day. Desi smiled up at the sky, "See, the Gods are favoring us today, no rain!"

"We are lucky, aren't we? No umbrellas to carry." agreed Sharon as the bus pulled up beside them.

Soon after their visit to the downtown shopping Mall, they stepped through the entrance doors of the restaurant and were immediately greeted by Pierre, who bowed to Desi and took her hand in both of his. "My darling, Desi. It is so good to see you again!"

Sharon and Desi had visited the restaurant often enough that Pierre had put them on a first-name basis. Desi giggled into her other gloved hand then shyly pulled off her blue wool beret and crushed it into her bag. "You are too, too sweet, Pierre. I will surely miss my visits."

"You are going away?" asked Pierre, leaning toward Desi as he led them to their favorite table by the windows.

"Not too far. I'm just returning to my Island home. But I'm not leaving until January."

"Well, I am glad that you are here today," he smiled and held Desi's chair for her to sit down.

While waiting for their lunch, Sharon and Desi giggled together over their Santa photographs. "Oh my, I look like I'm drunk - my hat was starting to fall off, and my hair is hanging over my eye."

"But look at how colorful we are - you in your pretty blue suit, Santa in his red and white, and your precious white curls match his beard."

"It's a good picture of your pretty smile. It will be perfect in a frame beside my bed, to remind me of all the fun we have been having."

"We have a couple of weeks yet before I drive you back home - I can get my neighbor to make a nice wooden picture frame to match your bedroom furniture. It's his hobby and he just charges for the material."

Their pre-lunch glass of wine had relaxed them into leaning back onto the comfortable brocaded chair cushions. They both enjoyed good appetites and had always ordered dessert. Pierre catered to their every wish, ready to serve them before they even thought of calling him. When it was finally time to get up and leave, Desi laughed as she momentarily lost her balance, "My goodness, I think I am drunk."

Sharon reach over to grab her arm, giggling, "Maybe we should sit a bit longer?"

Pierre appeared immediately at Desi's side taking her elbow and hand, "Can I offer you another cup of tea?"

"No, no, my sillies, I'll be fine. Just put me on the train, and I'll nap all the way home."

Sharon and Pierre looked at each other, grinning. "My aunt is a going concern, I don't know where she gets her energy from."

"She is a delight to see, so full of life and so cheerful." Pierre held the door open, followed them outside, and taking Desi's hand and bowing slightly, whispered "I will miss you, my dear. May I wish you a very Merry Christmas and a wonderful year ahead until we meet again."

Desi touched her lips as she blushed. "Thank you so much, Pierre, you make me feel like a giddy schoolgirl. Merry Christmas to you too, my sweetheart."

Watching her Aunt, Sharon's heart filled with tenderness and a quiet understanding of the loving connection that her Uncle and Desi must have enjoyed together. Thinking of Desi's loss of a sixty-year connection brought a tear to Sharon's eyes, as she took hold of Desi's elbow and dainty hand to help her down the step to the street.

CHAPTER 17

The following Friday would be the annual office Christmas party, held during business hours so that attendance by every staff member would be mandatory.

Chatting in the coffee room with Anna on the Monday before, Sharon had admitted that she had been hoping to avoid the event, "I haven't been to an official gathering for over three years."

Anna touched the back of Sharon's hand which was clutching the armrest of her favorite recliner, "Don't worry Sharon, it's been kind of fun the last few years."

"Do we need to dress up, or anything?"

"Some of our fashionistas change into fancy clothes, but I just go as I am. Last year the students all wore Santa hats, and Doug Burns came dressed as Santa Claus."

"We don't need to bring gifts, do we?"

"No, but Doug hands out our Christmas bonus envelopes."

"Well, that's a good reason to go," laughed Sharon as they got up to return to their desks.

The remainder of the week passed quickly, everyone seeming more relaxed than usual. Sharon had extra time on her hands, and used it to re-organize her desk, and allow herself moments to spend in conversation with chatty passers-by.

She had learned that the Christmas party included enough finger food to replace lunch, but to allay her nervousness about eating in front of all the lawyers she had amused herself on the morning of the party by taking quick hidden bites of Desi's lovingly prepared sandwich while trying to appear busy at her desk.

Just before noon, Anna walked toward Sharon's desk, grinning, "Okay, Sharon, time to enter the lawyers' cave."

Sharon sat up, eyes wide open, grabbing a tissue from the Kleenex box on her desk and wiping her mouth, "Oh yikes, is it that time already?"

Anna laughed, "What were you doing under your desk like that?"

"I, um... nothing. Is my face red?" Sharon couldn't keep the grin from her face.

"You do look a little pink, are you okay?"

Noticing that Betty was still at her desk finishing up her cigarette, and Julia was putting on lipstick, Sharon glanced up at Anna, "We've probably got time for me to run to the little girls' room first?"

"I don't feel like rushing all the way down there in this tight skirt," Anna grimaced as she yanked down on the sides of her skirt, "I'll see you in there when you get back."

After Sharon had checked her reflection in the lounge and was on her way down the hallway toward the coffee room, she saw Betty come around the corner, walking slowly toward her and their mutual destination.

Noticing the frown on Betty's face, Sharon thought, "Betty looks as unhappy as I feel about this party". She waited at the door until Betty had arrived, then smiled, "Hi Betty." As she opened the door to the coffee room, she mumbled to Betty, "Don't we just love these command performances?"

Betty grunted as she turned to follow Sharon, "Love isn't the word I would use."

"Well, let's get it over with." She took a big breath and sighed, "Maybe Doug will give out the envelopes right away and we can leave."

Betty nodded at Sharon and they both walked toward the door leading into the library. Betty held the door open for Sharon, waving her through with a quiet "After you."

Everyone seemed to be fully engrossed in their own group, balancing paper plates and wine glasses in their hands. Sharon stood beside Betty, "I haven't been to one of these for ages."

"I hope to avoid them from now on" answered Betty.

Sharon turned in surprise, "You're leaving us?"

"Yup, moving back to the Island for semi-retirement and to be closer to my mother."

"I didn't know you had family on the Island?"

"Grew up in Campbell River. Always knew I would end up back there."

"My Aunt lives on the Island too. I hope your mother is well?"

"She's fine, in her seventies now, but we both prefer Island living."

"Where will you be working?"

"It's a little one-man operation in Bowser. I'll just be working a few days a week."

"Bowser, I think I pass that place on my way to my Uncle's. I didn't think it was big enough for a lawyer's office."

"He works out of his home, and I'll be able to do a lot of the work at home on my own computer."

"It sounds like an ideal semi-retirement."

"Well, I like to do some volunteer work too, so now I'll have more time for that."

"I wish you the best of luck in your new..." Sharon noticed Santa Clause entering the library from the door on the opposite side, "Oh, here come the envelopes!"

"Thank goodness" Betty said under her breath, as she turned away from Sharon and moved toward the crowd gathering at the opposite door.

Sharon, left standing alone, turned to one of the empty chairs set around the perimeter of the library, sat down and wondered what to do with her hands.

Moments later Anna sat beside her in the next chair and handed her a glass of wine. "Here, I brought you a glass of your favorite Pinot Grigio."

"Anna, you are such a dear, thank you very much."

"I saw you talking to Betty. It looked like she actually agreed to a conversation for a change."

"Yes, until Doug opened the door, then I was cut off like a loose thread."

"Good for you. Did she have anything interesting to say?"

"Did you know that she's moving to the Island?"

"I'm not surprised, actually, she didn't seem to like Fisher much."

"Anyway, I didn't get a chance to find out when she is leaving or anything."

"I just hope they get a non-smoker to work for Fisher."

"Yes, and someone with enough spunk to keep him in his place, too,"

"A non-smoker, big, ugly and mean, that's what we need." laughed Anna as she finished off her glass of wine.

Sharon and Anna relaxed in their chairs, enjoying a few moments of idle chatter as they glanced around the room. Seconds later, Sharon's glance changed to a wide-eyed stare beyond Anna's profile, "Oh God no, he's coming over here."

She grabbed Anna's arm, "Let's stand up."

Anna put her glass down on the small table to her left as she turned to see the object of Sharon's frown. Standing up, she pushed down on the sides of her skirt, and bent over to brush the front of her low-cut draped blouse. She started to straighten up, her ample bosom still in view, just as Michael appeared in front of them.

His eyes flashed down to Anna's soft curves, just before he reached out to shake her hand, a grin just beginning at the side of his mouth as he turned to Sharon. Anna didn't let go of Westbrook's hand, and put her left hand over his as she moved slightly toward him, with a playful grin on her face, "Mr. Westbrook, sir."

Westbrook's amusement twinkled in his eyes as he disentangled his hand and made the slightest of movements toward Sharon. "Nice to see both of you here." Looking back and forth between them, he asked "You're not leaving already are you?"

Sharon couldn't help herself, she got the giggles. She took Michael's outstretched hand, holding her other hand over her mouth. "Not just yet, but I'd like to thank you, Michael, for the party."

"Yes, me too," Anna put her hand on Westbrook's arm and bowed her head in mock subservience. "We thought it best to honor you by standing in your presence."

"Please, I don't deserve any honor, I'm just glad you came."

Anna continued with her playful pose, "I'm very curious, Michael, has your new secretary answered your prayers?"

Michael grinned and mimed an inspection of Sharon, from her shoes, up to her hair and back down to settle at her eyes as he confided, "I think so, but time will tell. She's still pretty skittish for now."

Sharon put both her hands up to her cheeks, wishing she could disappear into the floor. She looked at Michael, her eyebrows raised while she stood speechless.

Anna seemed to be relishing the playful awkwardness, announcing, "Aha, I knew it, you have a new pony that you are trying to train, and she's not cooperating?"

Westbrook responded, laughing, "Well, she's new to these stables, she'll need time to trample down the hay in her stall and learn how to kick up her heels."

Anna couldn't resist, "Maybe she just needs more oats, green ones."

Sharon finally spoke up, cheerful annoyance in her voice, "Now just a minute you two. I might just kick up my heels and go galloping away to the food if you don't stop."

"Okay, ladies, you win." Michael threw up his hands in surrender, "Let's go. There's lots to eat at the other end of the room."

Anna fluttered her long eyelashes, tilted her head to the side and grinned at Michael, "My dear Mr. Westbrook, do we look like we need more food?" She stroked her fingers across her chest.

Sharon grabbed Anna's arm, leading her away from Westbrook with a whisper, "Honestly, Anna, you'll get us into more trouble than I can handle. You're outrageous."

"Well, who's being a mother hen, protecting her big lawyer man?" Anna laughed. "He can handle it, believe me."

"Come on, let's get something to eat. I'm starving."

Anna stopped mid-step, smiling at Sharon. "You can't be starving. I saw you eating that sandwich."

CHAPTER 18

Christmas was just around the corner. Sharon enjoyed this time of the year, the crowded shopping centers teeming with anxious faces. She welcomed the familiar rain-slicked city streets filled with vehicles crawling between signal lights, their wipers slapping back and forth, their back seats piled high with full shopping bags. She loved the tiny colored Christmas lights twinkling around windows and doors in every neighborhood.

On her lunch breaks she walked to the downtown mall, as much to watch the children on their Christmas school breaks, dragging their parents to see Santa, as to look for holiday treats and gifts for Desi. She loved the dark fruit cakes and Christmas candy that appeared only at this time of the year, buying extra so that she could enjoy them long past the season.

She and Desi had taken evening drives to admire the Christmas displays in the suburban homes described in the newspapers, Christmas music playing on Sharon's car radio. Having Desi staying with her this winter had been heartwarming for Sharon, making her realize she didn't want to be alone any more. It also made her more concerned about Desi living alone in her seaside home, which now seemed like a world away.

The day before Christmas, as Sharon and Desi sat to enjoy a glass of wine after dinner, Desi announced, "Well, I've finished all my shopping and other business, and we're going to have our very own turkey dinner tomorrow, with all the trimmings and candied yams.

"Oh Desi, that's so much work for us to do. Wouldn't you just like to relax tomorrow and we can go out for dinner?"

"No, my dear. I have been so happy for the last few months, I wanted us to have a special day together. Besides, I've done most of the preparing ahead of time, and it's a small turkey so we won't need to get up early to put it into the oven."

"I don't know where you get all your energy. You did all that today?"

"I've been going out almost every morning, just doing a few things at a time. Then I come home and have a little afternoon nap, and it feels like I can start all over again."

"Ah, yes. I know how much a small nap can help. The girls at the office all know I'll probably doze off during our morning coffee breaks, they even joke about it."

"Donald always took a short nap, nearly every day." Desi paused, a wistful look in her eyes.

"It certainly didn't do him any harm, with all the things he was able to do."

"He sometimes joked that the Mexicans had it right, with their daily siesta time."

Concerned that Desi would start feeling melancholy, Sharon jumped up "Oh, I forgot about the pretty table centerpiece I bought. Let me get it out so we can enjoy it right away."

As Sharon carried the bag back to the table, unwrapping as she walked, Desi reached for it, saying, "That looks lovely. Let's light the candles now."

"Good idea, I love the smell of Christmas candles."

Desi smiled, "We'll have a lovely cosy day tomorrow." Her eyes twinkling at Sharon, she said "Best of all, we'll have a real Christmas dessert."

"Oh-oh, my sweet tooth heard that word." laughed Sharon. "What will it be?"

"I found an old-fashioned plum pudding and the sauce for it too. I just couldn't resist."

Sharon leaned over to kiss Desi's cheek, "You're such a sweetheart. If this keeps up, I'll need to go on a diet."

On New Years Eve, Sharon and Desi wrapped themselves up in their warmest coats, hats and scarves and took the transit train downtown. Desi, with her tiny angora-gloved hands up to her face, her eyes bright with glee, seemed to enjoy the annual fireworks and music display. Sharon took a deep breath of the frosty night air as she soaked up the excitement of a new year beginning, the start of a new path in her journey.

She hugged Desi as they listened to the countdown to midnight, "Isn't this crazy?" She laughed, "We'll both need to sleep in tomorrow morning."

Desi tightened her arm around Sharon, "This has been so special for me. I'm not tired at all."

As they rode the train home, the low hum of the wheels and the gentle rocking of the coach had their effect. Sharon smiled as she leaned closer to Desi, whose eyes were drooping, her head nodding. "Just rest your head against my shoulder, we'll be home soon."

Sharon had felt the calming effect of Desi's companionship for the past few weeks, and had started to feel more contented and positive about her own future. She no longer doubted her ability to finish her law degree, she knew she could do it, even if she had to continue working between semesters. This was a new year, and she was ready to make the most of it.

The early days of winter passed by, Sharon back at work, Desi happily planning their evening meals, both of them ignoring the gloomy, rainy days. Although Sharon felt that Desi should stay in town until the worst of winter was over, Desi was determined to be back in her island cottage by mid-February.

"Well, my dear, the day has arrived," announced Desi as she and Sharon sat enjoying their morning coffee.

"Yes, I know," sighed Sharon, "I still wish you could stay longer."

"I'll be fine, really. And I've got lots to do in my garden." Desi paused, "I phoned my neighbor, Elizabeth last week, and she said everything is fine."

"That's Mrs. Reynolds, isn't it?

"Yes. She is so kind and she agreed to check my property while I was away."

"That's good. I remember that one year when it was so windy, a bunch of heavy branches had fallen down across your driveway."

"That was a terrible year. Donald had to hire people to come in and saw up the wood to clear our way."

"Well, at least we won't get any nasty surprises when we get there."

"I'm glad you decided to take a week off. That way you will see that I am well settled before you come back home."

Sharon had decided to make the week as trouble-free as possible. She had paid the extra fee to reserve a space on the ferry to the Island and she relaxed as she and Desi rode the freeway to the North Vancouver terminal, knowing exactly what time she needed to arrive. Although it was a Saturday morning, the ferry wasn't as crowded as it was during warmer weather. Winter travel had its advantages.

Sharon and Desi took the elevator from the car deck to the main passenger level of the ferry, and immediately joined the small lineup for the cafeteria lunch. Sharon lifted her head back, sniffing, "Oh, that smells good." She smiled at Desi, "I'm dying for some of that yummy clam chowder they serve"

"Me too." Desi reached into the dessert shelves and brought out two small plates of heavily-iced carrot cake, grinning at Sharon as she placed the plates on the tray, "and we'll still have room for cake with our tea."

"And we won't need to feel guilty, because carrots are good for us," laughed Sharon.

"We are so much alike, my sweet girl." Desi touched her gentle hand to Sharon's, "I'll go find us a nice table, if you can manage this tray alone?"

"Good idea. Would you like a dinner roll with your chowder?"

"No thank you, love. Just a few crackers will do." Desi patted her own stomach, "Must leave room for my dessert."

As she watched Desi walk to a table next to the windows, Sharon smiled, thinking to herself, "She's such a cute little thing, no wonder we get looks when we're together".

Before taking a seat, Desi turned to wave at Sharon, tilting her head to question the location. Sharon winked and waved her "perfection" gesture back at Desi, nodding her approval.

Sharon jumped when she heard a familiar male voice behind her, calling out, "Well, well. Look who we have here."

Sliding her tray toward the soup counter, she turned to follow the voice.

"Oh my God. David." She smiled past the two people immediately behind her, "What a coincidence."

"Or a small world," David grinned, as he reached out to shake Sharon's hand. "Happy to see you in a more relaxed world." The couple in front of David waved him ahead while they argued over the dessert selection. Moving up closer to Sharon, he whispered, "I'm glad I saw you. It's more fun to eat with friends."

"Well, I guess that's an invitation I've just been forced to give," Sharon chuckled. "I'm sure my Aunt will be happy to meet you."

"She's saved the best table in the room." He looked on as Sharon lifted the two bowls of chowder from the top of the counter. "Is that all you are having? You'll starve to death."

Sharon rolled her eyes. "Do I look like I'm starving?"

"Well your Aunt is a tiny little thing, maybe you don't feed her enough?"

Sharon watched his mischievous grin widen into a full smile, and realized that she had never seen that gleaming row shining directly at her. She had a sudden view of those teeth devouring a huge hamburger in two bites, and lowered her eyes quickly to avoid laughing. "We eat enough to keep us happy, don't you worry."

"Well, I want to pay for your meals. It's the least I can do for the enjoyment of your company." His eyes told Sharon he was serious, although his smile said otherwise.

"That's very sweet of you, David, but totally unnecessary." Sharon touched his arm before she picked up her tray and turned toward the cashier. "We'll see you back at our table."

David dropped his tray onto the top of the counter and ran ahead of Sharon as she slid her tray toward the cashier. "Here, I'm paying for this lady's meal," he announced to the cashier as he pulled his billfold from inside his jacket breast pocket. "I'll pay for mine when it's ready."

Sharon smiled at the cashier's raised eyebrows. "I guess he wins this one," she said. "Some people are just so stubborn." She turned to David and curtsied ceremoniously, pulling the sides of her jeans like a skirt, "Well, thank you kind sir."

She picked up her tray and hurried to Desi's side. While she moved their food and utensils onto the table, Sharon whispered as she smiled at Desi, "We're going to have uninvited company for lunch, I hope you don't mind."

"Ooh, this is exciting." Desi's face took on an impish grin, as she whispered "Do you suppose he has been following us?"

"I hope not, that would worry me." Sharon placed the tray on the empty table behind her and glanced quickly to see if David was finished at the counter. "It's David Westbrook, the student lawyer at my office."

"It is? My goodness, you didn't tell me he looks like an angel." Desi leaned forward to watch as David walked toward them. "Here he comes."

Sharon sat down beside Desi and turned to smile at David. "I thought it best to give you the whole side of the table for yourself, those broad shoulders need the room.

"Well now, I get lunch companions and compliments too? I must be doing something right."

"David, this is my Aunt, Desi Dunsmore." Turning to Desi, she murmured, "and Desi, this is David Westbrook, one of the articling students at the office."

David bowed and extended his hand, "So pleased to meet you, Mrs. Dunsmore."

Desi giggled as she curled her fingers over his, "It is my pleasure to meet Sharon's office companions. I have heard so much about all of you."

David widened his gaze as he sat down, "Aha, a beautiful French accent, my dear. May I ask from where?"

Desi's eyes fluttered as she blushed, "I was born in France, but I had been living in Montreal for several years when I met Sharon's uncle, my dear departed Donald."

David looked from Desi to Sharon, "Well that explains the difference between you two."

Sharon spoke up, teasing David with "What difference?"

David didn't skip a beat, "She's a tiny little lady with blue eyes and curly white hair."

"And I'm...?"

"Very tall. Very dark brown eyes. Legs like a pony."

Desi laughed, "Sharon was right. You do say surprising things."

"Yup, that's my game, keep 'em off balance, to remember my name."

Sharon looked up from her soup, "All right, you two. Time to eat lunch."

"Okay, I'll get serious if you insist." Pausing, he turned to Desi, "I hear that you live on the Island, Mrs. Dunsmore?"

Surprised at his question, Sharon blurted out "How did you hear that?"

"I was talking to Teri. She told me that you were taking your aunt back to the Island."

Desi glanced at Sharon. "Yes, it's my home. I love it there." Touching Sharon's hand, she smiled, "and I think Sharon does too."

"My favorite get-away, for sure," Sharon said as she returned to her soup, wondering why David and Teri would be talking about her. Looking up at David she tilted her head to the side, "Come to think about it, David, what is the reason for your trip today?"

"Oh, I want to check out the possibilities for opening my law practice on the Island, maybe up around Campbell River, after I'm finished my articling year."

Desi put down her spoon. "That's delightful. It's a lovely district and right on the water. Do you plan to make a permanent home there?"

"Yes, eventually, once I get settled." Glancing at Sharon, he said "I never did like big city living, and it's perfect for boating and fishing."

Sharon grinned at Desi, "We love sitting on Desi's front porch with our afternoon tea, watching all the boaters and fishermen sail by."

Desi squeezed Sharon's fingers, smiling. "My niece has been such a help to me since Donald passed, and we both love our tea and cookies. You must come to visit some time."

After they had finished lunch, Sharon wanted to get away from David. "Well, Desi, shall we do our usual walk?"

"But of course, we must get our exercise and see who else is on the ferry."

The ferry had been almost full, and for the first few miles after they had disembarked in Nanaimo, Sharon's fingers tapped on her steering wheel in impatience at the slow-moving traffic. Once they had reached the main highway, she sighed with relief as she stepped on the gas, saying "Finally. We're clear to go." She glanced at Desi, "We can stop at the grocery store just before your place, to stock up on groceries."

"Yes, that's a good idea. Then we can just relax at home for a few days without having to go out."

As they drove up the highway, Desi remarked, "This new highway is very fast."

"Yes, we bypass all the little waterfront towns this way."

"I do miss that old drive." Desi sighed, "Donald and I always enjoyed going that way. But of course we were never in a hurry."

"If you like, we can go that way. I like seeing the water too."

"Oh, that would be so nice. Let's do it."

After they had been on the old waterfront highway for a while, Sharon glanced at Desi. "I had forgotten how relaxing it is, going this way. I'm glad you reminded me."

"Well, I'm glad you are enjoying the drive." Desi was silent for a moment, then turned to Sharon and placed her hand on Sharon's arm. "I have something I want to tell you."

Sharon looked at Desi in surprise. "You do?"

"Yes. I learned a lot after Donald died, and decided to look after his money the way he did."

"That's good. He was very careful, and made sure that you were well looked after."

"Well, I wanted to do the same thing, so before I came to stay with you, I changed all my accounts and investments so that you and I are joint owners."

Sharon almost drove off the road. "Oh Desi, you should have talked to me first."

"Now, let me finish." Desi turned in her seat to sit up straight. "I went to see the lawyer in Courtenay and told him what I wanted to do. He helped me to set everything up so that you will be a joint owner but you won't need to report anything, and it won't cause tax problems for you."

Realizing the magnitude of her aunt's gift, she exclaimed, "Oh, my goodness, Desi. I don't know what to say. Thank you so much."

"Well, you can thank me if you are still alive after I die. If you die first, then my Will gives everything to the charities."

"Yes, you're right." Sharon looked with surprise at Desi, "I had no idea you understood all that when we were settling Uncle Donald's estate."

"Well, I mostly understood, but the lawyer had to help me by explaining everything when I asked how to fix things."

"And you didn't even tell Mr. Fisher when you saw him at my office?"

"I told a little white lie, that's all, when he asked if I had a joint owner on any of my assets."

"Oh, dear."

"Don't worry, it will all work out fine. Besides, it's none of his business.

"So everything is all set up?"

"Almost. You and I need to see my bankers because they need copies of your identification and such. We'll have lots of time for that next week."

Shortly afterward, their supply of groceries in the trunk, Sharon turned off the highway down to the unpaved roadway leading into Desi's property. "Well, everything looks good in here," Sharon remarked as she drove slowly along the roadway through the trees.

"Oh my, there must have been some snow here." Desi pointed toward Sharon's left window. "See, there's a bit still left over there in the shaded part."

"Well, I'm glad you were staying at my place while it snowed over here. I worry about you all alone here in bad weather."

"Here we are, Home Sweet Home." sighed Desi. "Let's get the fireplace started and put on the kettle for tea."

Sharon pulled their suitcases and the grocery bags out of the trunk, "That sounds so inviting. I'm glad we bought the banana loaf."

CHAPTER 19

While Sharon and Desi enjoyed the weekend of afternoon tea, and cozy evenings in front of the fireplace, a gentle old soul resting in his hospital bed at a long term care facility was soon to be dispatched far before his time. His room contained only a side table, the moveable table for his meals and two wooden chairs. Other than occasional visits from a volunteer helper, he was seen only by the doctors and staff of the facility.

After knocking softly on the door, the worker entered the hospital room, dressed in the standard uniform for repairmen and janitors at the facility, including the gray baseball cap. A heavy tool belt hung over the gray pants.

The gruff voice muttered, "Just need to check a few things, Mr. McGowan, I'll be quiet."

The frail, white-haired man turned his head on his pillow and lifted his fingers to signify he was aware of the visitor. He reached up to touch the tubing under his nose, as if to adjust for comfort, then slowly moved his long, bony fingers over his high forehead and through the sparse hair on the top of his head. He grimaced as he let his arm plop down beside him, worn out from the effort. He lay still, closing his eyes, until he heard the sounds of a step-ladder being opened.

"Sorry, sir. I won't be long." The worker's eyes, behind the goggles, glanced over at every movement of the patient. "Need to check the door and sprinklers and make sure alarms are all working."

A few minutes later, the worker stepped out in the hallway, then returned and set a small metal object on the floor at the end of the bed. Glancing at the sleeping figure while picking up the folded ladder, the worker stepped through the door and pulled it closed, making certain that the door latched without a sound. An ear to the door confirmed that the invalid occupant remained asleep, his soft snore barely audible.

CHAPTER 20

When Sharon returned to the office ten days after she had left it, it was with a heavy heart. She had left Desi early Sunday morning to board a morning ferry back to the mainland, struggling to hide her worry and sorrow. She had telephoned Desi Sunday evening, more to reassure herself that Desi wasn't regretting her decision than to express her own regret on returning to an empty apartment.

As she walked through the reception area, she could see that Teri was fully engaged, her head down, her left hand pressing her headset against her ear.

She reached over the counter to wiggle her fingers at Teri. It was their silent alternate "hello" to each other when Teri was busy with the phones.

Sharon reached her own desk, her tummy grumbling after she had passed the inviting coffee aroma from the staff lunchroom. She could hear Fisher yelling from behind his closed door. She looked over at Anna and noticed her sombre look.

"What's going on, Anna?" She took a few steps to cross the hallway towards Anna.

Anna looked around, paused for a moment, then murmured, "You have missed a week from Hell." She pulled her reading glasses off her nose and folded them toward her stomach. "I'm starting to feel like I'm the only sane person at this end of the office."

"Oh my God, Anna. I've never seen you look so serious." Sharon moved over to the desk of Fisher's assistant and rolled the chair over toward Anna's desk before sitting down. "Give me some papers to hold so it looks like we're talking business, while you tell me what has happened."

"I'm so glad you're back. Julia is on holiday so you and I are the only ones left down here."

"You mean Betty has left already? I thought she still had another week."

"She phoned in sick last Monday and hasn't shown up since. Fisher has just lost it, he's acting like a maniac."

Sharon sat up straight, amazement in her eyes, "Just because Betty's not here?"

"Maybe, but I think it's also because some old client of his died and the police are involved."

"Oh, no." Sharon's mind was racing. "Did you hear any details?"

Anna grinned as she lifted her glasses back into place. She leaned forward, "Fisher got me to do a Wills search when he got the Death Certificate on Friday, so I had a chance to peek through the file."

"What did you find out?"

"Well, the old guy, McGowan was his name, was another one of those clients with no family, a ton of money, and a Will that appointed Fisher as Executor. The Will gives almost everything to some charities."

"So why is Fisher so upset?"

"That's the crazy thing. The old guy must have really liked Fisher. His Will gives him a hundred thousand."

"Well, that's a good thing, isn't it?" Sharon paused, "Wait a minute. You said the police were involved?"

"Yes, but I'm not sure why. I overheard Fisher say something about suspicious circumstances."

"You mean like the old guy didn't die of natural causes?"

"I guess so."

Fisher's door slammed open. Sharon jumped up from the chair, dropped the papers onto Anna's desk and turned toward her own work station on the other side of the hallway. Fisher almost ran into her as he hurried toward the file cabinet beside Betty's desk.

"Sorry, Mr. Fisher, let me get out of your way. Can I help you with anything?" Her eyes widened as she noticed his disheveled hair and bloodshot eyes.

"Oh. Hi, Sharon. Welcome back." He stood up straight and ran his fingers through the hair hanging over his forehead. "Thank you. Would you mind digging the McGowan file out of Betty's cabinet? I need to get down to the police station."

"Oh my." Sharon hurried over to the cabinet, thankful that the files had been arranged alphabetically, and handed the folder to Fisher, a questioning look on her face.

Fisher glanced at Anna, then back to Sharon. "I don't know how long this will take. Would one of you please make sure my appointments are canceled or referred to somebody else?" He didn't wait for their response as he ran back to his office and emerged immediately, juggling the folder as he put his arms through his overcoat and hurried down the hall.

Sharon looked at Anna, "Was there anything on the news or in the papers?"

Anna shook her head, "No, not a thing."

At the end of the day, Sharon packed up her things early, to join Teri as they took the elevator down to Teri's car. Sharon waited until they had passed through the garage gates before asking, "Teri, what's going on with Fisher and the police?"

Teri laughed, "I knew you would ask. Something is definitely up."

"You're telling me! I've never seen Fisher look so frantic. When did this all start?"

"Well, I'm not sure when Mr. McGowan actually died, but we got a call from the care home early Monday morning, asking for Fisher."

"Fisher personally?"

"Yes. Well, I think he was named as the next-of-kin or the first contact person in their records. McGowan had appointed Fisher as his Power of Attorney a few years back when his C.O.P.D. got worse and he had to go into long term care."

"Oh, so maybe that's why the police want to talk to him?"

"I think it's more than that. I've heard that the old guy died of smoke inhalation."

"In a care home? They all have smoke detectors and sprinklers and stuff."

"That's just it. Apparently his room had been tampered with, and the nurses couldn't get into it when they saw smoke curling up from under his door. When they finally broke down the door, there was nothing they could do."

Sharon let the news sink into her mind for a moment, then glanced at Teri, "Surely they don't think Fisher had anything to do with that."

"No, but the police are probably trying to find out who would have wanted to get rid of the old guy."

By Thursday of the next week, things had become almost normal in Sharon's corner of the office. Fisher had introduced his new assistant, Vivianne, to Sharon, Anna and Julia.

That evening, as they drove away from the downtown, Sharon asked, "Teri, have you heard anything more about the Fisher and McGowan file?"

"No, not a thing. Fisher did look very relieved when he came back from the police station."

"We met his new assistant today. Did you see her when she came in?"

"Yes, she sat for a few minutes up front, waiting for Burns to come and get her. I think she'll be perfect for him, sort of a no-nonsense type of person."

"She looks to be about fifty."

Teri grinned as she glanced at Sharon. "Well, guess who gets to sort the mail and read job resumes that come into the office?"

Sharon chuckled. "Teri, you devil. You know all about her, don't you?"

"Yup, sure do." Teri took a full breath, "She's married, has two children in university, worked fifteen years at Russell and company, took a couple of years off to nurse her husband through some kind of illness, doesn't smoke, has lived in Vancouver all her life and has no plans to move."

"Wow, all that was in the resume?"

"No, silly. I just encouraged her to chat while she was waiting for Burns."

She winked at Sharon.

The next morning, Sharon's normal routine of attaching the day's incoming mail to the corresponding file and taking it into Westbrook's office was disrupted by Fisher's howl. She had seen Vivianne take Fisher's mail and files into his office several minutes before, and she suspected the uproar from his office was related to that delivery.

Fisher came flying headlong out of his door, glanced into Westbrook's empty office and came straight to Sharon's desk, holding a file in one hand and waving two sheets of paper in the other.

Sharon noticed that the papers were rattling in Fisher's shaking hand. It was a marked departure from his usual morning antics to amuse the assistants with a joke or silly story.

Sharon look up, smiling "Good morning, Mr. Fisher. How can I help you?"

He lifted his eyes to Sharon, looking almost surprised at her greeting, then smiled, "Okay, I get it. I need to calm down, right?"

Sharon hid her smile behind her hand. "You don't look like my favorite storyteller this morning, that's all."

"Well, today's story is a mystery to me." He put the sheets on Sharon's desk. "We've got another problem like that one you and the students have been working on."

"You mean the Boyle file, where another Will was signed after she got you to do a Will?"

"Yes, that's the one." Fisher's face lit up, "What's happening with that?"

"I guess that's another mystery. The lawyer who did the new Will couldn't reach the person named as Executor or obtain the original Will which was being held by the Executor. I think the charities are in the process of trying to knock the new Will out of the way. I'm surprised you haven't already heard about it, because you'll probably be the Executor for Mrs. Boyle's estate, under the original will you prepared."

Fisher paused, as if letting the information sink in. "I'd better have another look at that file. Are the students still holding it?

"Yes, it's been a real education for them."

"By the way, do we know anything about the Executor or beneficiary of Mrs. Boyle's second Will?"

"I don't know. The lawyers for the charities might."

"Well, if the charities get the whole estate anyway..." Fisher hesitated, then grabbed the sheets from Sharon's desk. "I need to contact the police about this."

Sharon looked up in surprise, "Why, what's happened?" She noticed Fisher's feet seemed planted to the floor, as if he didn't know which way to turn.

Fisher pushed his hair off his forehead as he looked at the papers. "This Wills Search Report says that Mr. McGowan did another Will about a year ago, so the one we prepared for him over three years ago has been revoked and probably names different beneficiaries."

"Oh, I see. The police only have the information about our Will, where the beneficiaries were mostly that Scottish society and another charity."

"Yes, so now they'll need to find out who will benefit from this other Will."

Sharon reached out to the papers in Fisher's hand, "Let's see who did that new Will."

Fisher handed the papers to Sharon, like a cook trying to get his hands off a hot handle. "Looks like a Notary Public out in Richmond somewhere."

"Hmm." Sharon handed the papers back to Fisher. "I guess that Notary will have the shock of his life, police showing up asking questions."

"At least I'm off the hook for now." Fisher turned hesitantly and stepped back toward his office, muttering, "I hope."

Sharon jotted down the name she had seen and slipped the scrap of paper into the small zippered pocket on the front of her purse.

Later that evening, Sharon pulled out her little phone directory and leaned back in her recliner while she dialed her former co-worker's number.

"Hi, Elaine, this is Sharon. How are you?"

"Well, I'll be darned." Elaine answered. "It's so good to hear from you. Have you got your law degree now?"

"Not yet. I'm back working at our old salt mines for a while. Have you got a minute?"

"Sure. I was just relaxing before I start my dinner. Got stuck at the office late again."

"I won't keep you long, then. So, no regrets about leaving the legal assistant world and becoming a Notary?"

"Are you kidding?" Elaine laughed. "It's the best thing I've ever done. Running my own show, keeping my own hours. The freedom is wonderful, even when I need to work late. You'll see, once you get your law degree."

"That's if Westbrook doesn't get me to give up. He seems to think I should just get married and have kids."

"Westbrook? You're working for Westbrook?" Elaine paused, "He's talking about marriage?"

Sharon laughed as she realized that Elaine's voice had shrieked up an octave.

"No, never. He just keeps making sarcastic remarks about my time off to keep up with my courses."

"You poor thing. He's probably the worst one to work for in that office."

"Oh, I'm coping." Sharon cleared her throat, "Anyway, there's been a whole lot of weird stuff happening, and that's why I'm calling. Do you know anything about a Notary in Richmond by the name of Erkstine?"

"Sure, that's Bernie. He's been a Notary forever. He was our leader when we were being trained to deal with wills and estates. That's his specialty."

"That's good to hear. He'll probably be getting a visit from the police about a Will he did about a year ago."

"He will? What's that all about?"

"Apparently the old guy's death is being investigated as suspicious. Fisher was all prepared to probate the Will he did about three years ago, and he had to tell the police who the beneficiaries would be. Then he found out there was a more recent Will, prepared by Erkstine, and had to tell the police about that one instead."

"Oh my God. Bernie's going to have a fit." Elaine paused. "Well, there won't be anything wrong with the Will that's for sure. Bernie's a real stickler for details."

CHAPTER 21

Many days passed, most of them with Michael away at Court working on a trial that was expected to last for at least six months. Sharon had started working more and more for Michael's son, David. She had heard that Michael's original secretary did plan to return from her sick leave, and Sharon had more or less decided to continue working for David, as he seemed more than willing to make allowances for the extra time off she needed. She had taken two more of her law school classes during the Spring semester, and by the end of June felt exhausted and ready for a holiday. She knew the ideal place to get away and relax.

Waiting for Desi to answer the ringing phone, she felt a little jump of excitement as she thought about the ferry trip and a relaxing visit with her Aunt. Finally she heard Desi pick up her phone. "Hi Desi. How are you?"

"Hello my darling. I'm absolutely wonderful now that I am hearing your voice."

"Would you like a visitor for a couple of weeks?"

"You can stay for a holiday?" Desi squealed in delight. "Oh, that is the best news ever!"

Sharon could almost see Desi clapping her hands, like a child being told she was going to Disneyland.

"I just need to work for another week and I thought I'd come over on the Thursday before the July long weekend to avoid some of the holiday traffic."

"Oh, I'm so happy. I'll go shopping so we can have some of our favorite dinners."

"Now don't you go wearing yourself out. We can go shopping when I get there."

"I will love being busy and planning." Desi paused. "I'm going to start my list right now."

Sharon laughed, "Now you're starting to sound like me, with my lists."

Desi chuckled, "Yes, this old poodle can still learn new tricks."

"So, it's all settled then. We'll have a good visit."

"I can hardly wait."

"Me too. We'll talk on the phone again anyway. Let me know if there is anything you want me to bring over with me."

After their conversation, Sharon pulled her suitcase out of the storage cupboard and opened it onto the floor in the corner of her bedroom. "This way I won't forget anything, I'll just throw in my stuff as soon as I think of it. First is my bathing suit and beach mat."

The next day at the office, Sharon walked into David's office. "Good morning, Mr. Boss Man. How are you today?"

David looked up at her. "Okay." He paused. "Something's up, I can tell." as his smiling eyes widened. "So, what's on your mind?"

"I'd like to take the first two weeks of July off." She sat in the chair facing his desk. "I'll get all your work completely caught up to date, and you probably won't miss me at all." She smiled.

"You have no idea how I'll feel, believe me." He leaned back in his chair, grinning, and folded his arms across his chest. "You're running off to get married or something, right?"

Sharon couldn't prevent the shocked look on her face, "David, what a thing to say. You sound just like your Dad."

"Okay, I'm sorry. Just teasing. Dad told me you were touchy." He unfolded his arms. "You probably just need a holiday."

Sharon took a big breath. "I'm heading over to the Island to stay with my Aunt for a couple of weeks."

"Oh yes, Desi." He leaned forward in his chair. "I met her with you on the ferry last February, right?"

"Yes. She is my only aunt, and we both enjoy getting together."

"I liked her. What did you say her last name was?"

"It's Dunsmore, the same as my mother's maiden name."

David picked up his pen, "That's Dunsmore, just like it sounds?"

Later that morning, after Sharon and David had reviewed his files and work load, Sharon sat down and prepared a detailed summary of each item requiring attention, in their order of urgency.

That evening, as Sharon rode with Teri on their way out of the downtown traffic, Teri looked over at her. "You look beat, my dear. Had a rough day?"

"Well, it's sort of self-inflicted. I'm trying to get David's work completely up to date before I take off for two weeks."

"That sounds familiar," laughed Teri. "Work like a slave so you can take a holiday, then come back and work like a slave to catch up."

Sharon smiled, "This is a crazy business, isn't it?"

"You bet, but at least we never have a chance to get bored."

Sharon leaned back against the headrest. "I'm heading over to visit my Aunt, hoping to find some peace and quiet. A bit of boredom might be good."

"Good for you. The weather is supposed to be good for the next while. You might even get some beach tanning time?"

"Sure hope so. Desi has regular afternoon naps, so I'll probably get lots of time to lay around."

"How is she doing? Still as cute as ever?"

"She's doing really well. I think she's finally adjusted to my Uncle being gone. She seems to be reaching out a bit more, neighbors and sociable stuff.

"Good for her. She seems like a real sweetheart."

After a few more days of constant activity, Sharon's longed-for Wednesday ride home arrived. "Well, I did it." Sharon sighed as she settled herself into her seat in Teri's car.

"Well, you've sure done something, kiddo. I haven't seen you on a lunch or coffee break all week."

"It was worth it. Now I can take my holiday with a clear conscience."

"You spoil those two men. Michael has even boasted about what you do for him and David."

"Really? He sure doesn't let me know how he feels. I have yet to hear a 'Thank you' from him for anything."

"If it's any consolation, I've noticed a big change in Michael since you came on the scene. He seems way more relaxed now."

"He certainly talks a lot to David, though. I've heard more of his comments second-hand through David than from Michael himself."

"So you and David get along okay?"

"David's fun, and he treats me like an equal. I like working with him for now, but I'm still going through with my law degree. I don't want to be a legal assistant forever."

"You go girl. I can see a great future for you."

"Thanks, Teri, you're such a good friend. Don't know what I'd do without our ride home after each day."

"Well, hopefully the next two weeks will fill up your bucket again. You deserve a good rest."

"I've got all my packing done, so I'll be up early tomorrow morning to catch the ferry. I just love getting on that ferry."

"A nice relaxing way to start your holidays."

CHAPTER 22

The next morning, Sharon was out of bed, into her most comfortable jeans and T-shirt, and half-way along the highway to the ferry terminal before she realized she had forgotten to turn off her radio alarm. She had set it to wake her at 7:30, but was already on the highway by 7:15 am. For a moment she considered turning back, as she felt guilty about her neighbors hearing her radio playing for an hour every morning. She continued on the highway, however, after she rationalized that the radio volume was set at mid-range, and there would be no harm in making her apartment sound like someone was home.

Even though she lived in a building with secured entry, she still had an underlying fear of break-ins or burglary, especially since her husband had died.

Turning her thoughts back to her driving, she smiled as she thought about the familiar rituals of waiting in the long line-up of cars at the ferry terminal.

Most of the time, if she had missed a scheduled ferry because it was full before she had arrived, she had enjoyed walking to the indoor market for a snack or wandering through the tourist kiosks that appeared every summer. If time allowed she would walk to the water's edge and lean over the wharf's metal railings to watch seagulls and ducks in the oily water below.

Just being at the ferry terminal seemed to trigger a deep sense of relaxation in her and sometimes she spent the entire waiting time simply sitting in her car, reading the newspaper or a book, letting the sea breezes flutter the pages through her open window. She would look up occasionally to watch people with their bouncing pets and children wander about the parking area. Once boarding was allowed, even the bumpy, metal-clanging ride over several moveable ramps, into the dark innards of the car-devouring whale had become an enjoyable part of her holiday frame of mind.

Today's trip left no time to spare. She arrived at the terminal just as the next ferry was spitting out its motorized cargo, and the number of vehicles ahead of her in the lineup was relatively small. As she drove onto the ship, the familiar diesel smells and rumbling vibration of the lower deck seeped into her car, triggering an automatic restful response to her whole being. She relished the feeling of escaping from the world. In Sharon's imagination, the Island was a far-away land of flora and fauna, full of dreams, fairies and peaceful freedom.

Once the ship was under way, she packed her magazine, her purse and a small bag of bread crusts for the seagulls, locked her car and walked up the long flights of stairs to the upper decks of the ferry. She found a seat close to the large windows and sat down to wait for the ship to begin moving.

After the loud warning horn sounded, the ship shook with a heavier vibration as the propellers were reversed, to pull the ship out of its berth between the wooden planks. The seagulls abandoned their lookout perches on the tin-topped pilings to begin their flight alongside the big white whale.

As the ferry turned to begin its westward journey, Sharon picked up her belongings and walked to the door leading to the outside deck. After she struggled against the strong winds to open the heavy door, she squinted her eyes as the cool air blew her hair across her cheeks.

She walked out to the railing to watch the smaller boats outside the docking area scurry out of the way. After the ferry had completed all its maneuvering and was well on its straightaway toward the Island, Sharon opened her bag of bread crusts and held out torn-off pieces for the seagulls. Their ability to fly close enough to the swiftly moving ship to snatch the bread from between her fingers had always fascinated her, and this time was no different.

Within a few minutes, a few children had gathered around to watch, and they giggled with glee when Sharon gave most of the bread to them so that they could also enjoy the mid-flight feasting.

A short time later, after she had devoured a breakfast of scrambled eggs, bacon, pancakes and a coffee, Sharon found her quiet window seat still unoccupied. She curled her legs up beside her and as she started to leaf through her magazine she could feel sleepiness starting to creep up into her eyes. Thinking she could just doze for a few minutes, she relaxed.

The announcement directing passengers back to their cars on the decks below woke Sharon with a start, surprised that she had slept through most of the journey. She jumped up, grabbed her belongings, and joined the lineup of passengers waiting to go down the stairs.

Getting into her car, she yawned and stretched, then rubbed her face to feel more alert. Watching the cars in the line ahead of her, she waited until she saw their taillights shine before she started her engine, not wanting to add more fumes than necessary to the already smoky atmosphere of the lower car deck.

A few minutes later she was cruising along the highway, enjoying the flow of cool fresh air through the open windows and feeling more relaxed with each passing mile. She loved the peaceful look of the small farms along the way with their big red barns and fields of swaying grass filling the spaces between the cheerful beach tourist towns with their flower-lined boulevards and hanging baskets.

By the time Sharon slowed down to turn into Desi's roadway, she felt completely free of the city and any thoughts of studying, working or deadlines. At the end of the slow winding dirt road, the sight of Desi standing on her back patio among the flower-filled terracotta pots, her arms outstretched in welcome for Sharon, brought tears to her eyes as she smiled and waved, then turned to park behind the garage.

Desi opened the car door before Sharon had shut off the ignition. Moments later, after their hugs of greeting, they moved Sharon's belongings out of the car, chatting as if there had been no interruption in their conversation or companionship.

The days of Sharon's first week with Desi were filled with fun and laughter.

They traveled to their favorite garden shops and public markets, walked along the beach and through the shops of the small towns along the highway and scoured through the treasures of neighborhood garage sales. In the evenings they sat on the front porch to watch the twilight settle over the ocean, as they chatted and shared their stories of neighborhood or office gossip.

"Are you still working with that nice young man I met on the ferry last February?"

"You mean David?" Sharon replied. "Yes, I've been doing a lot of work for him over the last few months. He's a full-fledged lawyer now, so he can get his own clients and make more money than he did as an articling student."

"He seemed like a real gentleman." Desi smiled, a twinkle in her eye, "I think he likes you."

Sharon could feel a blush warming her cheeks. "Well, we do have a lot of fun working together. He is always making me laugh."

"I'm glad to hear that. Your Uncle was like that too. He was always making me laugh at something." Desi turned to gaze at the ocean, as she let out a soft sigh.

"I miss him too." Sharon reached out to touch Desi's hand, smiling. Trying to keep cheerful, she bubbled, "Didn't we all have fun together, all those visits we had?"

Desi moved to face Sharon, her blue eyes wide and enthusiastic. "Yes, you're right. We made some wonderful memories, all of us. Now it's your turn to start working on new memories."

Sharon sat forward in the patio chair, "Now, Desi," she smiled, "You and I are making new memories all the time. I love the visits we have, and the cruise we took was the best holiday ever for me."

Desi seemed determined to have a serious conversation. "But I want you to think about more than just holidays with me." She reached her hand to Sharon's. "You are such a beautiful girl, you shouldn't be alone, and I won't be around forever."

Sharon sat speechless for a moment. "Desi, why are you talking like this? Are you not feeling well? Are you worried about your health?"

"Oh no, my dear." Desi clasped her hands together at her chest as she giggled. "I'm as healthy as a horse, and full of beans as well. I just think you and David would make a perfect couple and your children would be gorgeous." She paused. "There, I've said it. I've been thinking about you and him for weeks now."

Sharon laughed. "You little monkey! I hope you haven't done anything mischievous."

"Now, Sharon, you know I wouldn't do anything silly. I don't want to be a busybody, but I do love to dream about happy endings."

"Well, my life could be a fairy tale, but I'm not sure David is interested in being my knight in shining armor."

Desi leaned back in her chair and murmured, "Life is a gentle journey, full of surprises."

By the next weekend, summer temperatures were warming the whole Island, and both Sharon and Desi had become content with relaxing through the noontime heat. Desi cozied herself with reading in the hammock on the shady front porch, and Sharon packed her beach supplies through Desi's front gate and down to the beach to suntan.

Sharon had her favorite spot, her back resting against a large driftwood log, a book propped up on her knees, with her large floppy sunhat shading her face. If she got too warm, she would walk into the chilly water and swim over to the neighbor's wharf, satisfied that she was doing something healthy for herself. Afterward, the peace and quiet would lull her into sleepiness, and she would roll over to expose her back and legs to the warm sunshine.

Desi's property was wide enough to make the beach very private, with the edge of the neighbors' properties at least 100 feet away on each side of her.

By Tuesday, Sharon had spent four afternoons at the beach, and was starting to think about what kind of adventure she and Desi could enjoy for the remainder of her holiday. Little did she know that fate had other plans for her.

She had cleaned up the kitchen after she and Desi had enjoyed another of Desi's creative lunches, and they had both agreed that they would have one more day of napping the early afternoon away. Sharon had spent a few minutes reading before she slid down onto her beach blanket to close her eyes and soak up the sun.

She wasn't certain how long she had been there when she felt a coolness on her shins, as if the sun had gone behind a cloud. She lifted up the brim of her hat, and at seeing white denim-glad legs above a pair of white sneakers, she flung herself up into sitting position and found herself looking up at David, with his hand lifting his white baseball cap in a form of greeting.

"Whoa, there, pony girl. It's just me." He chuckled, "Those arms and legs could be weapons at that speed."

"David, what are you doing here?" She motioned to the log, "Here, sit down so I don't need to look up into the sun." As she grabbed her beach coverup and threw it over her shoulders, David walked toward her and held out his hand.

"Come sit up on the log beside me. Feels more equal that way." He smiled as he turned toward her, propping one knee on the log in front of him, his other foot in the sand.

"I can't believe this." Sharon couldn't keep the happy shock from her face. "How did you find me, and how did you get here?"

"I've been out on my sailboat all weekend, and yesterday when I was looking through my binoculars at this shore, I saw you walking out the gate and setting up your stuff on the beach."

"Wow, what a coincidence."

"Not really. I knew your Aunt lived up in this area."

"You looked her up in the phone directory?"

A sheepish look flickered across his face. "Sure, why not? Why shouldn't I be able to find my best legal assistant ever?"

"Did you come in from the highway? Through Desi's property?"

"Hey girl, don't I look more like a sailor than a driver?"

"Oh." Sharon grinned. "I guess I've been out in the sun too long. You're right, I would have heard you coming through Desi's gate." Sharon turned to look at the neighbor's boat dock. "Oh my God, is that your sailboat?"

David stuck out his chest in playful pride. "Yup, that's my lady. Isn't she a beauty? My summertime home on the weekends." He waited until Sharon had turned to face him. "Want to go sailing?"

Sharon ignored the question and reached up to take off her hat and fluff her hair. "I want to take you up to see Desi, she won't believe her eyes." Sharon bent down to gather up her blanket and tote. "I'll take all this stuff back up to the cabin now. Enough tanning for one day."

"Here, let me carry some of that for you." David took the blanket from her arm, gave it a shake and folded it before reaching down to pick up her sandals.

As they walked up the garden pathway to Desi's front porch, Sharon motioned with her finger to her lips and whispered, "I think she's probably sound asleep inside the hammock." As they reached the step, Sharon called softly, "Desi, are you awake?"

A sudden movement of the hammock followed by Desi's hand and white curls appearing above the edge made Sharon giggle.

David smiled as Desi pulled herself into a lounging position. "That's quite a cozy cocoon you're curled up in there, my lady."

"Oh, my goodness. It is you." Desi rubbed her eyes, "I was having a dream about you and Sharon."

"I hope we're not upsetting your dream." David reached out to Desi's hand, "Here, can I help you up out of there?"

Desi grinned at Sharon, "See, I told you he was a gentleman."

Sharon took Desi's other hand as she swung her feet up over the edge and down to the porch floor. She asked Desi, "Shall I make us all a cup of tea?"

"That sounds yummy. I'll get out my banana bread too and we'll have a real afternoon tea." Desi slipped her feet into her fuzzy mule slippers and clapped her hands as she scuffled in through the open french doors, Sharon and David right behind her.

Later, as Sharon tidied up the dishes after their repast, David continued to chat with Desi. "You and your husband certainly chose an ideal retirement location. Did you enjoy boating as well?"

Desi clasped her hands to her chest, "Oh goodness, no. Neither of us were sailors, especially after the time his sister and brother-in-law took us out for a holiday on their boat."

David laughed. "The look on your face tells me it was a fearful experience?"

"The waves were bigger than his boat, and I got seasick. I thought we were all going to die."

"It must have been a sudden storm that came up, people don't usually go boating in bad weather."

"Oh, yes. It was the last day of our holiday and we had to cross the Straights to the marina where he kept his boat."

"So you all made it home safely, though?"

"All I can remember is being on my knees down in the eating area, praying for all I was worth. I had to hang onto the steps to keep from falling over."

Desi chuckled to herself. "My other hand was holding my throw-up bucket. The worst part was Donald, covering his mouth to keep from laughing at me."

"So he didn't mind boating?"

"Well he did drag his rowboat down to the water sometimes to go fishing, but he never insisted that I join him, thank Heavens."

"I was hoping to take you and Sharon out for a little sail this afternoon. There is a mild breeze, but the water is very calm today."

Desi jumped up from her chair and walked over to Sharon. "Sharon, my dear, David would like to take you out on his sailboat. Let me finish cleaning up."

Sharon looked from Desi to David and back again. "Desi, you look all flushed, are you okay?"

"I'm fine, I probably just got up too quickly." She took the dishtowel from Sharon's hands. "Now you two just run along for your boat ride. I'll stay here and fix my special chicken dinner." She turned to David. "I hope you will stay for dinner after sailing?"

"Thank you so much, Mrs. Dunsmore. Sharon and I can sail down to the marina at Schooner Cove and bring back a dessert from the hotel, if you like?"

"Would you be able to do all that by dinnertime? By six o'clock?"

"If that's when dinner is, I'll make sure we're back in time." He hesitated, "Oh, I just thought about where I've docked. There was no answer when I knocked on their door."

"Oh, you'll be fine there. They are away on their boat until the middle of August."

"They won't mind if I leave my boat there again when we come back for dinner?"

"No, not at all. They've asked me to check on their place once in a while. They're good neighbors."

David turned toward Sharon. "Okay, my dear. We've got the go-ahead from your aunt." He glanced quickly down to Sharon's feet. "You'll probably want to cover up a bit more and maybe wear sneakers or some other soft-soled shoe."

Sharon smiled as she saw the glee in Desi's eyes. "She's got me married off to him already." she thought to herself.

A few minutes later, as David turned his yacht to head south and turned off the engine, Sharon sighed in wonderment at the sudden silence. "This is heavenly, all I can hear is the breeze pushing the sails."

"I gather your Dad's wasn't a sailboat?"

"The noise from the diesel engine was all I could hear when I went out with Mom and Dad. This is so much more peaceful."

"And environmentally friendly, too, I might add." He reached out to Sharon. "Come here, take the wheel for a few minutes."

Sharon's eyebrows shot up. "Oh my God, no. I'll capsize us, I'm no sailor."

"Well, now is a good time to learn." He put Sharon's hands on the large wheel at the back of the boat and stood behind her, with his hands just below hers.

"We're heading a bit into the wind, so we'll need to tack back and forth a bit to make headway."

Sharon could feel the warmth of his chest at her back, and a tremble starting in her arms. She took a big breath and straightened out her shoulders. "Okay. I'm okay. How do we 'tack'? I don't even know what that means."

By the time they were approaching Schooner Cove, Sharon had felt confident enough at the wheel to let David climb up toward the bow and take her picture.

"You get back here now, mister. We're getting close to some land up ahead."

David laughed as he bounced back down to the deck beside her. "Hey, you did really well. We could have some fun this summer."

Before Sharon could react, David had reached down to restart the engine.

"Now, what's next?" she asked him.

"You just keep our heading toward the end of the jetty there. I'll go pull down our sail and put the bumpers over the side. Then we'll just coast into the wharf."

"I'd rather you steer. I watched you put up the sail, so I think I can get it down again."

"That's a girl. A mind of your own."

On their way back up toward Desi's home, the wind was behind them, making the trip much quicker and uneventful. Sharon felt much more relaxed, content to sit on the cushioned bench beside David while he stood at the wheel.

Although the relative silence between them felt comfortable to Sharon, she couldn't resist the temptation to get David talking. "I've heard that you've spent a lot of time in other parts of the world. I'd love to hear about your travels sometime."

"I'm glad to hear you say that. I do have a few good stories to tell."

"Do you have a favorite place?"

"Funny you should ask. I think I've finally found the ideal location." He picked up his binoculars, then reached down to start the boat's engine. "Okay, my matey, time to pull down the sail again."

While working with the sail, Sharon glanced back at David and noticed a slight smile on his face. Climbing back down beside him, she asked, "I don't mean to be nosy, but where might that location be? I'll bet you want to be somewhere close to your father?"

"Well, Dad sure gets riled up about me making the best use of my life., but I think he really just wants me to settle down and 'get a life', as he calls it."

"Wow, that surprises me." She looked at David's profile. He didn't look upset. "How do you feel?

David shrugged. "He's probably right. I think he would probably like it best if I produced at least three grandchildren for him and lived in a big house with a basement suite for him and my uncle."

Sharon was speechless. Was David talking about the same man that Sharon had been working for? She stood up to look ahead, toward the focus of David's attention. "Oh, look. Is that Desi's place up ahead?"

"Sure is. Better go hang the bumpers over the side before we land. Get ready to use your land legs again." He smiled as he glanced down at Sharon's feet.

A few minutes later, as David guided the boat toward the neighbor's wharf, he announced. "Okay, kiddo. Go get the bow line and be ready to jump onto the wharf to tie us up."

Sharon scrambled forward, picked up the bow line and bent over to hold the railing as she straddled it, waiting to get close enough to the wharf. She heard the engine shut down just as the boat glided into place.

Jumping onto the wooden planks, she reached out to hold the boat from hitting the rubber bumpers on the side of the wharf as she watched David tie down the stern line.

After working together to secure both shore lines to the wharf, Sharon and David strolled over toward Desi's front gate. Sharon turned to him, "Thank you so much, David. That was quite an adventure for me."

David reached down to unlatch the gate and hold it open, waving Sharon through. "Aye, aye, m'lady. It was my pleasure, my seafarer's desire, to bring the treasure to shore."

Sharon laughed, "Now you sound like someone with a black eye patch and a wooden leg. And it's only a lemon pie."

As they walked the cobblestones through Desi's front garden, David reached out and put his hand around Sharon's waist. Sharon gulped, feeling her heart skip a beat. "Oh my God, I'm a goner!" Afraid to say anything, she sighed with relief as Desi appeared at the French doors, her arms wide open with a welcoming smile on her face.

"There you are, my two sailors. How was your trip?" Desi reached out to take the box from Sharon. "And what do we have here, something good to eat?"

David spoke up. "I hope you like lemon pie. It looked too good to resist."

By early evening, after they had finished their dessert and moved to the front porch, Desi had succeeded in getting enough information about David's world travels to satisfy most of Sharon's curiosity about his past. Sharon reached over and patted Desi's knee. "Well, you two seem to have a lot in common." She smiled at both of them. "I feel like I've been watching a promotion for world travel."

Desi clasped her hands together, "Oh my dear, this has been a wonderful day for me. It almost feels like Donald has been with us to enjoy revisiting all those places." She turned to David, "I hope we can have other visits. You have had such an interesting life."

David reached out to hold one of Desi's hands, "Mrs. Dunsmore, I will be happy to visit anytime you wish." He turned his smile to Sharon, "If your niece doesn't object."

Sharon didn't know what to say as she glanced at her watch. "Should I put on the kettle for an after-dinner cup of tea?"

David's response, as he stood up, surprised her. "I think I'd better get on my way, if I'm going to get back before dark."

Sharon stood up. "I've just realized I don't know where you've been staying."

"I've been moored at a small Marina near downtown Nanaimo. I'll be heading back to Vancouver by Thursday." He turned to Desi. "Thank you for your gourmet dinner, Mrs. Dunsmore, it was delicious."

"You're welcome, David." Desi's face lit up with pleasure. "I really enjoyed cooking for a man again."

David chuckled. "Glad to oblige." He turned toward the steps and glanced at Sharon and Desi, "Would you like to bid me farewell from the wharf?"

Desi giggled, "That sounds so romantic!" She turned to Sharon, "My dear, you go with David to watch him sail away. I'll stay here and tidy up the kitchen."

"Now Desi, you know I won't let you clean up all by yourself. You just sit here until I come back." Sharon turned to follow David as he strode toward the gate. He stopped at the gate and waved back at Desi, then repeated his welcoming wave and posture to Sharon as she caught up to him and walked through. She could feel a sense of loss starting to grow in her chest as they walked toward the neighbor's wharf.

"What are those sad eyes thinking about?" David asked as he jumped in front of Sharon and walked backward as he bent down to look at her, a big grin on his face.

Sharon put her hands up to her face. "Now I'm embarrassed. I'm just being silly, I guess." She continued toward the boat. "It's been fun today, and I haven't seen Desi so happy in a long time."

"You're very close to your Aunt, aren't you?" David's gentle words as he turned to walk beside her almost brought tears to Sharon's eyes.

"Yes, she's really the only family I have now." Sharon cleared her throat and looked up at the sky. "The sun is starting to go down. What if it gets dark before you get to Nanaimo?"

David chuckled, "Now that's a typical landlubber question if I've ever heard one."

Sharon whacked at his shoulder. "I'm a sailor now, remember? At least in the daytime. I did okay, didn't I."

"Yes, you made a good First Mate. I might just hire you." He held out his hand as Sharon stepped up onto the wharf. "See those lights on the boat? They're required for all boats out on the water when it gets dark. The left side of the boat must show red lights, and the right side has green lights."

"Oh, I see. That way you can tell which way a boat is heading, even if you can't see the boat."

"Hey, you're a quick study. Good for you." He bent down to untie the bow line from the cleats on the wharf and handed the line to Sharon. "Here, you hold this until I get the motor started."

A few minutes later Sharon stood at the dock watching as David's boat backed away from the berth. When he was far enough away from shore, he hauled up the sail, then waved goodbye at Sharon before he spun the ship's wheel and turned his focus to the waters to the south. She stood there for a few minutes, her hand still up in the air, her throat aching.

CHAPTER 23

About a month after their boat trip, David called Sharon into his office.

They had settled into a comfortable office routine, to all outward appearances simply a lawyer and his assistant. Behind his closed door, he was just as likely to tease Sharon about getting her out on his boat again as to simply sit back in his chair in silence. Sharon had been pleasantly surprised at his willingness to hear her opinion on some of his files. She had been even more surprised at his understanding and encouragement of her plans for a law degree.

This day was different. David dropped a bombshell into Sharon's soul when he announced, "Well, it's official. I'll be leaving Stewart & Company in a few weeks. There's a small law firm on the Island that has asked me to join them."

He paused for a moment, looking directly into Sharon's eyes. "Now I'm wondering if a certain ambitious law student could be talked into moving to a small island town."

Sharon had not expected any change in her plans and her first inclination was to say "No," but she instead announced, "That's wonderful, David. I hope everything works out well for you. This law student needs to finish school before she can think about moving." She hadn't noticed the fleeting look of disappointment on David's face.

As the time came for David's final week at the office, he and Sharon worked many extra hours together, long after the office had emptied, packing up all his personal files and books into boxes. Teri, in her own teasing way, had expressed the certainty that there was a relationship brewing. "C'mon Sharon, working together all day and then he drives you home. You know that's gossip material."

Sharon laughed. "Don't you dare tell anyone that he's driving me home."

"Oh sure, they're going to believe that you take the transit train home after all these years of riding home with me."

As if to prove Teri's theory, David surprised Sharon with an invitation as they were finishing another long day. "C'mon Sharon, I'll take you out for dinner tonight before we take you home.

Maybe it was the wine they enjoyed before their dinner, or the fact that it was a Friday, Sharon felt more relaxed and ready to let down her guard with David that evening.

Knowing that he had made plans to move to the Island had made it easier for her to settle her feelings and accept the fact that David had plans that didn't include her. She had enjoyed working with him and wanted to continue their companionship. Taking another sip of her wine, she looked at him, "Well, there's one good thing about where you're moving to."

He smiled at her, "What? Besides the fact that the location has almost everything I want?"

"I'll be able to drop into your office whenever I come over to see Desi."

"Now you're talking" he joked. "That's more like what I want to hear. So, what are your plans once I'm out of here?"

"I'm going to take a few weeks off. Then I'll probably get back into temporary assignments around the city if Stewart & Company can't keep me busy enough."

"Have you registered at the University yet?"

"No, I've decided to apply in January for next September's classes, and in the meantime I'm going to sock away as much money as I can."

"You've only got one more year of lectures left before you can start your articling year."

"Yes, I know. I've been procrastinating long enough." She took a long breath. "I've decided to complete that last year of courses without interruption, even if I need to take out a loan."

David looked surprised. "So money has been the main reason you're not already finished?"

"That, and I hadn't really made my mind up about what I wanted to do when I grew up." Sharon smiled into her glass of wine. "Now it's time for me to 'get a life', as your father would say."

David grinned. "Sounds like my Dad has had an effect on both of us. He's be very proud if only he knew."

Afterward, during the ride to Sharon's apartment, she realized that this afternoon might be the last time they could relax together. "David, what do you think?"

He glanced at her, smiling. "About what?"

"Well, we've only got about half a day of work left. How about if we meet at the office tomorrow, finish everything up, and then have dinner at my place."

"I think that's perfection!" He reached out to pat her hand. "I'll bet your cooking is even better than your Aunt's."

"I'll get everything ready tomorrow morning, before I head to the office."

"And I'll pick up a bottle of wine to have with our dinner."

The next day was a whirlwind for Sharon as she concentrated on making everything as perfect as she could. It wasn't until early evening, as she and David sat at the dinner table like an old married couple, that she let herself feel calm. David seemed more relaxed than usual, and had surprised Sharon with more information about his family and his plans for the future.

"So, you're certain that the Island is where you want to make your home?" His hesitation in replying spurred Sharon's curiosity. "You've been to so many exciting places. Isn't it going to be too quiet for you?"

"No, I think it will be the opposite. It's got everything. Safe harbors, boating, good fishing, beaches, ski mountains, forests, lakes, rivers. Lots of healthy outdoor living."

"Probably a good place to raise a family too?" Sharon couldn't resist asking.

David grinned at her. "What do you think?"

After they chatted for a few more minutes, David looked at his watch and stood up. Sharon could feel that ache in her throat again. "Oh, is it that time already?"

"Hey, I guess we've been having too much fun, like that old saying about making time fly."

"Well, David. I am sure going to miss you at the office."

"I'm not falling off the edge of the world, you know. We'll be seeing each other again."

As they approached Sharon's door, David turned to put his hands on Sharon's shoulders. She stopped dead in her tracks, looking up at him and thinking, "I can't let him see my silly schoolgirl feelings."

"I know I shouldn't ask." He looked down into her eyes. "This hasn't been an official 'date', but I'd like to give you a big hug before I leave. You've been good for me."

Sharon reached out and pulled herself toward him, turning her cheek to rest on his chest. "David, you are so sweet. It feels like you've opened up my world. Maybe it's okay to have fun and be silly and enjoy life."

"That's the way it should be, my dear." He grinned. "You can't wear black forever."

After Sharon shut the door, she leaned against it and let herself slide down to sit on the floor. Her knees felt weak.

On Monday, Sharon did a quick check of David's now-empty office, to make sure it was ready for the next occupant. She knew that David was making the rounds to say goodbye to the people he had worked with. She wasn't surprised when just before she left for lunch, he approached her, his briefcase in his hand.

"Well, my dear. It's really official now. I am no longer your boss."

Sharon laughed, "You were never my boss. We just agreed on everything."

"Good one. You got me." He paused, "There's just one more thing I hope we can agree on."

"Maybe." she teased.

"That I can have your phone number?"

CHAPTER 24

By Thursday of that week, Sharon had to admit to herself that she missed David, surprised that she felt a longing to hear his voice.

That evening, Sharon was determined to relax as she sat in her recliner with her dinner on her lap tray, and her happiness sweets and amusements on the table beside her. Jumping slightly when her phone rang beside her, she lifted the receiver and mumbled "Lo?", through her mouthful of dinner.

"Hi Sharon, this is David."

She finished swallowing. "Does he really think I don't know his voice by now," she thought. "Hi David. How's everything going over there?"

David jumped directly into his question. "Listen, have you got any assignments for the next few weeks?"

"No, I was planning on just taking it easy for a while."

"Great, I need you over here, you can stay with my cousin and her husband, they have a nice basement suite you can stay in, I'll pay for the whole thing, including your transportation."

"David, I don't know what to say." Sharon could feel her pulse in her ears.

"Say yes. I need you to help me set everything up in my new office. They have no kind of system for anything, and you'd be the best person to get everything organized."

"Flattery now? You must be desperate." Sharon laughed.

"Besides, it's beautiful over here. The leaves are starting to turn, and the evenings are nice and cool."

Sharon grinned. "Now you sound like a tour guide." Hearing no response, she thought, "Oh darn, he's being serious." Clearing her throat, she said "I'm sorry David, I'm just being silly."

Before she could finish telling him that she would probably be able to help, David interrupted with "Good. I'll meet you at this end of the ferry on Friday night, say around five, and you can follow me to my cousin's place."

His positive approach got the desired results, and an "Okay" escaped from her lips, then "Just a minute, let me write this down."

"Ah yes, the ever efficient assistant, even in off-hours. Ferry terminal at five o'clock - you'll have to catch the 3:30 ferry on Friday."

That weekend was a whirlwind for Sharon. She met David's cousin and family, followed David around the supermarket while he threw food from both sides into the cart to stock the tiny kitchen she would be using. As he held up a box of frozen chicken wings for her approval, she laughed, "David, how long are you expecting me to stay? There's enough food here to feed an army."

"Well, you might have some company once in a while." He winked at her. Sharon spent the rest of the weekend like a tourist, as David took her to his new office and then gave her enthusiastic commentaries about each of the town's attractions and surroundings as they drove past them or stopped to enjoy. By Sunday night, Sharon was looking forward to a home-cooked meal. David had taken her to six different restaurants and snack bars in those two days.

The first week in David's office taxed Sharon's energies to the limit. He had given her free rein to do anything and spend whatever necessary to get him and the office totally organized. She brought in extra filing cabinets, set up a new filing system, lovingly chose a desk blotter and matching pen holder for David's desk, and spent long hours emptying boxes of files and law books until her back ached.

With the approval of David's two law partners, she also set up a computerized calendar program with all computers linked, so that all three lawyers, as well as their assistants, could view and plan their days and appointments.

On Wednesday of the second week, Sharon was surprised to see a 3:00 p.m. entry in the calendar system for a Mrs. Dunsmore. "That can't be Desi, she would have told me." she thought.

That afternoon Sharon heard a female voice from the reception area office say "I'm Mrs. Dunsmore, and I'm here to see Mr. Reese" The voice sounded vaguely familiar to Sharon but she knew it wasn't her aunt and carried on with the work on her desk.

A few minutes later, her curiosity aroused, Sharon took a quick stroll past the entrance to the waiting room. Seeing an elderly-looking woman sitting with her back to Sharon, with a head of thick white curls, she muttered "I must tell Desi that there's another Mrs. Dunsmore."

That evening Sharon telephoned Desi for their nightly conversation. Sharon and Desi had agreed that they would talk to each other every day, and that Sharon would spend as many weekends at Desi's home as she could. Sharon had an unspoken fear for Desi, living alone in her little house on the ocean side of the large wooded lot. Her previous delight in the peace and quiet was now being replaced by her worry over the remoteness of the place. "Thank heavens it's only an hour's drive to get there" she thought.

Sharon listened to the ringing tone as she propped the phone between her shoulder and ear. Thinking "Desi knows this is the time I usually call." Lifting her hand to hold the phone in place, she got up out of the armchair. A few more rings and she started pacing across the living room floor. "C'mon Desi, where are you?" She was about to hang up when she heard the interrupted ring and a soft, "Hello?"

"Desi! Are you all right?" The quiet at the other end of the phone made Sharon's heart stand still, her mind alert. "It's me, Sharon. Is everything okay?"

"I'm sorry, dear." Desi hesitated, as if taking a big breath. "I've been so sleepy lately, I didn't hear the phone ring until just now."

"You sound terrible. You were fine on Sunday morning when I left. What's happened since then?"

"Everything is just the same. I had a nice visit from my neighbor Elizabeth on Sunday after you left."

"That's good. Have you told her that you aren't feeling well?"

"Goodness, no. I'm just very tired, that's all."

"Have you been eating properly?"

"Oh yes. I've been eating the wonderful cabbage rolls that Elizabeth brought when she came to visit on Sunday. I'll finish them off for tomorrow's dinner."

Sharon noticed that Desi seemed to be slurring some of her words. "You haven't taken any unusual medicine or drinks or anything, have you?"

"Not really. I did have an extra cup of coffee this morning, but it didn't really help."

Sharon could feel the fear creeping up her neck. Her Aunt had used the word "help". Desi had usually been cheerful and positive when they talked, sometimes hiding negative thoughts behind a little joke and not revealing her troubles until long after her negative mood had passed.

"Well, maybe I'll drive up on Friday right after work."

"That would be nice. Then we will have two evenings together instead of just Saturday." Desi paused, then in her most gentle voice "I hope it won't be too rushed for you after working all day."

"Please don't worry about it. I might even leave work early so we can have dinner together."

"You are such a sweetheart."

"We'll talk again tomorrow night. I'll call earlier in the evening so that I don't wake you again."

After hanging up the phone, Sharon realized that she had forgotten to share her news of another Mrs. Dunsmore.

The next day Sharon dialed her Aunt's number as soon as she had thrown off her office clothes and pulled on her jeans and t-shirt. While waiting for her call to be answered, she glanced at her reflection in the mirror and tried to smooth out the wrinkles.

Walking into the kitchen, she reached down to get a saucepan and lid from the lower cupboard, pulled a tin of soup off the pantry shelf, used the electric opener, and poured the contents into the saucepan. Subconsciously keeping track, she suddenly realized that the ring tone had sounded at least fifteen times.

"Maybe I dialed the wrong number" she thought as she canceled the call and carefully dialed Desi's number again. "Still no answer." Sharon realized that she had said the words out loud.

"Darn, I don't even know your neighbor's last name." She held the wireless phone in front of her face and spoke at it. "Desi, please answer your phone." then returned it to her ear to continue listening to the hollow rings for a few more minutes.

Putting the phone down on the table, Sharon finished putting together her dinner of soup and crackers. Feeling distracted and uneasy, she poked at her meal while keeping her eye on the phone, hoping it would ring with a call from Desi.

After cleaning up the kitchen, she glanced at her watch. "I can't go rushing up to Desi's now. She'll get all upset with me for worrying about nothing."

Sharon waited an hour, then dialed the number again, with the same result as her earlier call. She turned on the television, but soon realized that she wasn't really concentrating. "Well, that's it, I need to do something."

She picked up her flowery note pad from the table beside her, propped her feet up on the footstool and held the pen poised ready to write. "First of all, I need to see Desi's neighbor, Elizabeth, to get her phone number. Probably should contact several of her neighbors so I can get someone to check on her if this happens again. And I'm going to buy her a cellphone."

After she had written a few more items on her list, Sharon felt more calm and ready for bed.

The next morning, Sharon arrived at the office early, thankful that David had been in the habit of starting work at seven every morning. He would be there to let her in.

"Hi, David" she bounced past him as he held the door open. "I hope you don't mind, but I want to get out of here early this afternoon."

"Hey, that's fine with me. It is Friday, after all."

Sharon rushed through the projects she had lined up for the day, and found her thoughts drifting toward Desi as she worked. "That reminds me, I must remember to tell her about the other Mrs. Dunsmore." Her early start to the day and her eagerness to finish her work as soon as possible had shortened the time it usually took for Sharon to use up her breakfast calories. Looking at her watch as her stomach growled, she decided to take an early lunch break.

Wanting to keep her mind active while she ate, and curious about the other Mrs. Dunsmore, Sharon took a quick look for the Dunsmore file. She knew no one would question her picking up any file in the office, whether it was David's or not, because of the organizing she had been doing for the office. She walked over to the desk of Reese's assistant. "I saw that a Mrs. Dunsmore had an after-hours appointment yesterday. Do you have the file?"

Cora looked up at Sharon, "Funny you should ask. I've just finished closing it. It's down in that box at the end of the hall, ready to put into storage."

"Oh, that was fast. Not much to do?"

"No, not really. Mrs. Dunsmore came in last December for a Will, and yesterday she signed a Power of Attorney that we prepared. I just used the same file for both documents, even though they were done in different years." Cora grinned, "And I did remember to add the details to the computerized client list you set up."

Sharon patted Cora's shoulder, and smiled, "That's a good girl, I knew I could count on you."

Sharon strolled down to the box, found the Dunsmore file, then walked to the back room where a table and chairs had been set up in front of the fridge and kitchen sink.

She dropped the file on the table, then pulled her lunch bag from the fridge and sat down, emptying its contents onto the table. She picked a few grapes off the bunch and squished them down into her yogurt, popping the remaining grapes directly into her mouth. Lifting up her yogurt in her left hand, she opened the file and leaned forward to read the contents.

Sharon almost choked when she saw the name and address of the client on the Power of Attorney. It was Desi's. "Oh my God, what is this?"

Sharon put down her spoon and yogurt container and started flipping through the pages in the file. "This can't be right. Desi was with me in Vancouver in December, she couldn't have signed this Will."

Looking further, Sharon found copies of a Driver's License and the government Health Care Card, both bearing Desi's name. The picture on the Driver's License was her aunt.

She shut the file and stood up, "I've got to tell somebody about this," as she turned blindly toward David's office.

"David, I think we have a problem." She plunked herself down in the chair facing his desk, then hesitated. "Oh, I'm sorry, David. I didn't mean to barge in, but do you have a minute?"

"For you I'll always have a minute. What can I do for you?"

Sharon's mind was racing, she could feel fear creeping through her hair. "David, do you remember that Boyle file you had at Stewart & Company?" She didn't wait for David's response, "I think there's a similar problem here, but this time I know this Will can't be my Aunt's."

"Huh?" David's eyebrows crinkled up his forehead. "Let me see the file. Is this your Aunt?"

"Well, the name and address, and even the copies of the ID documents are my Aunt's, but there is no way that she could have signed the Will that's copied in this file, and it certainly wasn't her that I saw in the waiting room on Wednesday."

"Could it have been her who signed the Power of Attorney last night?"

"I don't see how. I talked to her on the phone earlier this week, and she didn't sound well, and last night when I tried to phone her again, there was no answer."

"Why do you think this Will isn't hers?"

"Because she was with me in Vancouver all of December, and you saw how frail and elderly she was when we had lunch on the ferry. There is no way she would have been able to get to the Island and back to Vancouver while I was at work. And she wouldn't have made a trip like that without telling me."

David lifted the pages to read the Will. "Who is this Elizabeth Reynolds? She's described as a dear neighbor in this will, and her address is almost the same as your Aunt's"

"Oh my God, David. I didn't read that far. I have to get up to my Aunt's right away. I've got to talk to her about this."

"Now, calm down, girl. I don't want you to go racing up to your Aunt's in a panic. People change their Wills all the time."

Sharon took a big breath, "Okay. I'll finish my lunch and tidy up my desk."

"And watch the speed limit on the highway."

Sharon went back to her lunch, gulped down the remaining yogurt and shoved the other lunch items back into the bag, thinking "I'll eat the crackers and cheese on the way."

She stopped at her desk and gathered up the papers and files, throwing them all unorganized into the box on her chair. She turned off the computer, picked up her things and jogged out to her car, digging into her purse for her car keys along the way.

Throwing her purse and sweater into the back seat, she fell into the driver's seat and had the key in the ignition before both feet were on the floor of her car. She turned the key, revved up the engine, and left without waiting for the motor to warm up.

She was in a state of nervous apprehension at finding Desiree. Her phone call to Desi's number earlier in the day had been interrupted by the automated announcement that the number was not in service.

The drive up the island highway had a calming effect on her as the road wound its way through tall forests and past the beach front parks and resort properties. She knew she had to stay calm. She opened the electric windows as she drove, letting the wind whip her hair around, to keep her mind clear.

When Sharon knew that Desiree's property was only about a mile further up the road, she slowed down to the posted speed limit. Seeing the small clearing on the right side of the road that led into Desi's property, Sharon turned off the highway and down the slope to the beginning of the long curved driveway.

Although it was mid-afternoon, the rainclouds added to the darkness along the driveway. The grass growing down the center of the road between the tire ruts had apparently grown unchecked for a while on the heavily-treed property. Sharon could hear the occasional twig scrape under the body of her low-riding car and slowed to a crawl to avoid getting caught up on a bump.

As she rounded the first curve in the road, Sharon slammed on her brakes. She couldn't believe the sight in front of her. A huge cedar tree was lying across the road.

Looking at the size of the tree, she knew it was one of the oldest trees on the property. She cranked her steering wheel around and after several hurried forward and reverse movements, she had turned her car around to face the highway and backed it up to the fallen tree.

Climbing over the tree, Sharon was glad that it had been casual Friday at the office that day. Her jeans and sneakers were doing their job, leaving her unconcerned about her physical appearance.

With her purse swinging wildly behind her, she ran along the shaded, cool roadway. jumping over the grass median from one rut to the other as puddles blocked her way. She could see the gray brightness of the ocean ahead through the trees, and she was relieved when Desiree's little blue home, silhouetted by the sea, appeared at the end of the last bend in the road.

She slowed her pace, thinking out loud "I'd better slow down, I don't want to upset Desi by being all out of breath."

She finally stepped up to the back door and gave a timid knock, thinking that Desi might be having an afternoon nap. Hearing no response she tried the door. It was locked. She turned to her right and stepped down off the patio deck. Walking along the overgrown path that led to the front of the house she was surprised at the neglected state of Desi's treasured garden. Sharon thought, "Maybe the weather has been too cold for Desi the last few weeks."

As she walked past her Uncle's chimney of smooth rocks, Sharon reached out to stroke the cool surface. It was a habit she had indulged in whenever she passed the colorful tower, to remind herself of her Uncle Donald and his beaming pride over his unusual creation.

Reaching the front of the house, Sharon was again dismayed at the look of the yard, with weeds that were taller than the rose bushes. "Maybe I can convince Desi to hire someone for the heavy yard work." She took the two steps up onto the wide front porch, tapped a window of the French doors and stood waiting for a response.

She cupped her eyes to look through the windows, but could see no sign of life in the living room or kitchen. She had turned and was halfway back toward the steps when she heard a faint "Hello" from inside. She jumped back to the doors and knocked again.

A weak "Who's there?" came to Sharon's ears and after that, a low moan. Sharon wondered if her mind was playing tricks on her; it sounded like "Help me."

She bent forward to turn the handle, then pushed the door open a few inches. She called inside. "It's me, Desi. Are you okay?"

"Oh Sharon, thank God." Desi's faint words floated toward Sharon. "In the bedroom, dear."

Sharon pushed the door wide open and took three long strides to reach the open bedroom door. She rushed to Desi's bedside, moaning. "Desiree. Oh my. You poor thing. What's happened to you? You look like a ghost."

She knelt down and picked up Desi's thin listless hand, holding it between both of her hands, trying to transfer some warmth to the frail bony fingers.

"I've been so tired, I thought I was going to die" cried Desiree. "I can't stay awake."

"But why didn't you tell me when we talked on the phone?"

"I didn't want to worry you. It's just a few days that I've been so sleepy."

"I tried to phone last night, but your phone isn't working."

"I know, I tried to call the doctor."

"Have you eaten anything today?"

"No, the chicken stew is all gone."

"Chicken stew?"

"Elizabeth helped me at first. She thought I would finish off her cabbage rolls, so she brought me a big pot of homemade chicken stew for my dinners. She had to go away for a few days." Desi tried to get up on her elbow, "She brought me some fruit and candy too. She's been so kind."

Sharon fluffed up the pillow and tucked it behind Desi. "You just rest back. You don't need to get up. I'll be in the kitchen to fix you something to eat."

"I haven't been shopping for a while. I don't remember what's in the cupboards."

"Don't worry, I'll run to the store if I need to." Sharon turned and paused on her way to the door, "By the way, did you have a big wind storm here in the last week or so?"

"No, it's been very peaceful." After a few more breaths, Desi asked "Are the phone lines down?"

"I'm not sure." Sharon rushed into the kitchen. She didn't want to frighten Desi with the news that a tree had fallen over the driveway.

A short time later, Desi rested back on her pillow, a contented smile on her face. "That was the best cup of tea I've had in ages."

"Well, as long as the toast and soft-boiled egg stay down, I guess cookies and tea made a good dessert." Sharon pulled the padded stool from the vanity table and sat down beside Desi. "I'm going to phone your doctor for an appointment tomorrow, or if he's not available, we'll take you to the hospital. I think you should get some tests done, maybe you're anemic or something."

Desi lifted both her frail hands to her cheeks, "Oh dear me! I don't want to be a bother."

"You're not a bother. I can't leave you alone like this. You and I will need to talk about some changes." Sharon rested her hand on Desi's knee, "One thing for sure, we're getting you a cellphone, and I'm going to get the phone numbers of all your neighbors."

Desi let her arms drop to her side as she smiled at Sharon, her eyes looking very heavy. "Here I go again, off to dreamland."

"That's good, my sweetheart. You just rest and I'll work around the house for a while. I'll try to be quiet."

Desi mumbled, "I like your sounds." as Sharon tiptoed out the door.

Sharon tidied up the kitchen and left the dishes soaking in hot, soapy water. Noticing the pink glow of the sun against the mountains across the Straights, she thought, "I've got to check that tree before it gets dark. We'll need to clear it away."

She walked down the driveway to the fallen tree, and walked alongside the tree toward its thicker end. Expecting to see the tree end in a tangle of dirt and upended roots, she was shocked when she saw the glaring flat surface of its sawn-off stump. "Oh no. Somebody cut it down." Sharon's heart started to pound, as she turned and trotted back to the cabin.

Sitting down at the kitchen table, she rummaged through her purse for her cellphone, then reached for the phone book on the bookshelf beside her. Leafing through the yellow pages, she muttered to herself, "Let me see, it should be under gardeners or trees."

After arranging for the tree service company to come on the next Monday, Sharon dialed the number of Desi's doctor. After explaining her concern, Sharon was pleasantly surprised that he agreed to wait if she could bring Desi to his office right away.

Sharon went into the bedroom and touched Desi's soft white curls. "Desi," she murmured, Wake up, my sweetie, we're going to see your doctor."

Desi opened her eyes in surprise, then turned toward Sharon. "What did you say, dear?"

"I talked to your doctor. He's waiting for us to get there."

Desiree struggled to get up onto her elbow, and Sharon reached over to lift her and turn her knees to the side of the bed. Sharon ran to the closet and shoved the hanging clothes back and forth until she found a thick jacket. Wrapping it around Desiree's shoulders, Sharon helped guide Desi's shaking hands into the sleeves. "Now just sit for a minute while I find something for your feet.

Desi pointed to the closet, "My moccasins, they'll keep me warm.

While Sharon was slipping the soft sheepskin slippers onto Desiree's delicate feet, she remembered that her car was still out past the fallen tree.

"Desiree, sweetheart, I had to park my car half way down your driveway. We'll need to use your car to get closer to mine. Where are your keys?"

Leaving Desiree sitting on the edge of her bed, Sharon ran out to the garage and yanked up the overhead door. She jumped into the musty-smelling compact car and was surprised that it started immediately. Jamming it into reverse she raced out of the carport, swerving to back up to the steps at the edge of the back patio. Leaving the motor running and the passenger door wide open, she ran into the house.

Seeing that Desi had stood up and was leaning against her bedroom door Sharon rushed to her side. "Desi, you should have waited for me. You might have fallen." She put her hand under Desi's elbow and wrapped her other arm around Desi's back. "Let me help you. We'll just walk slowly. We'll get there."

A few minutes later, after Sharon had lifted Desi's knees and turned her to face forward in the passenger seat, she ran to the other side of the car and dropped into the driver's seat. She drove slowly over the bumpy, rutted road, glancing over at Desi for signs of distress, as she tried to keep the ride as smooth as possible.

When they had reached the fallen tree, she turned off the key, ran around to the passenger door and reversed her movements to get Desiree up out of the low-slung seat.

Desiree paused as she stood up, squinting as she looked past her car. "What's this?" She turned to Sharon, her blue eyes wide with surprise. "A tree down? How did that happen?"

Sharon answered "I don't know. Maybe it was old and the wind blew it over."

She felt guilty about her little white lie, but didn't want to worry Desi at this stage of their journey.

"Oh my, I can't climb over that tree. Is there room under it?"

Sharon smiled as she visualized both of them wiggling like worms to get under the tree. "No, we can't go that way. We'll manage. It will be our adventure for the day." Sharon lifted Desiree up onto the tree, "Now just sit there and hang onto this branch beside you. I'll climb over to the other side and help you down."

Desi turned so that her knee was resting on the tree as she watched Sharon reach to hug the tree and roll over to the other side. Desi giggled, "Oh my, that looks like my first try at horseback riding."

Sharon's worrying thoughts lightened as she realized that Desi was almost enjoying their adventure. "Well at least this horse isn't going to gallop away leaving us hanging on for dear life."

She lifted Desi to the ground. Desiree started to giggle, and in spite of her worry and concern, Sharon caught the giggles too. As they struggled together over the few feet to Sharon's car, Desi remarked "We must look like a couple of drunks."

Desiree's family doctor expressed shocked surprise when he saw her. "Well, we certainly must find out what's wrong with you. Let's take a look." He wrapped the blood pressure sleeve around her thin arm, "and then we'll telephone to see if we can get you a bed in the hospital right away. I think we need to do some tests."

Later, while making notes in Desiree's patient file, he spoke over the phone to the hospital admitting desk. After a few minutes, his frown confirmed the bad news, "There won't be a bed until tomorrow." Looking at Sharon, he asked "Will you be able to stay with her for the night and bring her down to Nanaimo General tomorrow morning?"

"I'll help any way I can," she replied. Helping Desiree with her jacket, Sharon gave her a big hug. "Come on, Desiree, let's go have some dinner before we drive back home. We can go to the drive-through so you won't need to get out of the car."

"I'm so sorry to be so much trouble, I don't know what I would do without you."

"You won't ever be 'without me' if I can help it." Sharon could feel the tremble through Desi's sleeve. "I just want you to be healthy again."

Driving from the doctor's office Sharon noticed Desi's eyes drooping. She pulled off the highway and reached over Desi's knee to recline the seat, then grabbed her trusty napping pillow and colorful afghan from the back seat. Tucking the pillow under Desiree's head then spreading the cover over her knees and shoulders, Sharon whispered, "There, you just lay back and rest. I think we'll just go pick up some groceries and go straight home."

Desiree's contented murmur confirmed her acceptance of Sharon's decision. Her gentle snore a few minutes later brought a sigh of relief to Sharon's lips.

Sharon knew there was no panic to get home. It would be much better to drive gently to the store and then to the property so that Desiree would continue sleeping.

When they reached the entrance to Desi's property Sharon shifted her car into reverse and inched it down from the highway and drove until its back bumper almost touched the fallen tree. Moving with extreme care to make no noise, she removed the groceries from the trunk and put them into Desiree's car. She opened the car door, reaching in to stroke Desi's hand, and called her name.

After shaking her head and rubbing her temples, Desiree looked up at Sharon and turned in her seat. Looking around her, she said "Oh, we're home already." A determined look appeared on her face.

Using her left hand on the door handle, and supporting herself with her other hand holding Sharon's, Desi managed to pull herself into standing position. She stood still for a moment, smiling. "I feel better already."

"Okay, Desi, are we ready for our next step?" Sharon wrapped her free arm around Desi. In a few moments, with both of them laughing, they repeated the sit and roll procedure to get to the other side of the fallen tree.

Once inside the house, Sharon helped her aunt into the darkened living room and onto the overstuffed armchair. She lifted Desi's feet onto the footstool, then grabbed an afghan from the couch and wrapped it over Desi's knees. "Now you just sit there like a good girl, and I'll fix our dinner."

Desiree sighed, "Oh, this is so cozy I could fall asleep right now." She rested back against the chair's pillowy headrest and turned to watch Sharon at the stove. "I'm so sorry to be this useless, Sharon. I haven't been able to do anything for the last few weeks, and I had such pains in my hands and feet."

"And you didn't say a word to me about it, you bad girl." Sharon turned her worried smile back to the stove, whispering to herself, "I knew I shouldn't be leaving you alone here."

"Now don't you start feeling bad. You have a busy job and I was sure my aches and pains would go away."

"Are your hands and feet still bothering you?"

"No, they stopped a couple of days ago. I forgot to tell the doctor about that."

"Well, he'll know by next week, after all the hospital tests."

"Elizabeth has been telling me that I would probably get better on my own. I was silly to let it go on so long, I guess."

After their dinner, Sharon settled Desiree into bed again, with clean sheets and freshly plumped pillows. She was cleaning up in the kitchen when a gentle knock sounded on the back door and a cheerful voice called "Yoo hoo. It's me, Desiree. I'm back."

"Oh Elizabeth, come in." Desi called from the bedroom "Sharon, please let Elizabeth in. I want you to meet her."

Introductions were made and as Elizabeth sat down on the stool beside Desiree's bed, Sharon returned to the kitchen. While wiping down the table and counter, she remembered that she should let David's cousin know that she wouldn't be back in her suite for a few days.

Sharon knocked softly on Desi's bedroom door. As Elizabeth turned toward the door, Sharon asked her "Would you mind staying with Desi for a few minutes? I need to get something from my car and then make a couple of phone calls."

"Certainly, dear, I can stay as long as you need me." Turning to Desiree, Elizabeth shook her head. "That daughter of mine is being so unreasonable these days. I was so glad to be out of the house last week. She's been living with me ever since she quit that job with the lawyer in the city, and she's been nagging me about this and that ever since, as you well know, Desiree."

"Yes, I'm sure she's unhappy about something. She certainly wasn't very cheerful the last time she came to visit me. When was that? I've lost all track of time."

"About two weeks ago, just before you got sick."

"Well," broke in Sharon, "I'll scoot out now and be right back as quickly as I can."

Later that evening after Elizabeth had left, Sharon sat in the bedroom with Desiree until she heard her first gentle snore. Sharon tiptoed out and sat down on the sofa to read for a while.

Finding only one small blanket and a couple of sheets, she decided against opening up the sofa bed. "I'll just cozy myself up on the sofa under Desi's afghans and keep my clothes on." she thought, grimacing as she imaged how wrinkled she would look in the morning.

CHAPTER 25

Sharon tossed and turned for a while after she had turned off the reading lamp. She soon realized that she was feeling hungry and got up to make herself a hot chocolate and bring it back to the sofa.

She leafed through a few pages of her magazine and was just dozing off again when she thought she heard a noise outside on the front porch. "It must be a squirrel or something" she thought, "my nerves are getting bad from lack of sleep", and she cuddled herself down into the blankets even more.

Some time later, she heard a small cough from Desiree's bedroom, opened her eyes slightly and was about to close them again when she realized that there was a red glow from outside, through the french doors.

All her senses jumped to panicked attention as she realized that there were flames outside Desi's bedroom wall, and smoke was starting to curl its way in above the french doors.

"Desiree, wake up, the house is on fire!" Sharon called frantically as she ran toward the bedroom door. Pushing the door further open, Sharon was immediately engulfed in a choking smoke that filled the room showing only a reddish glow in the direction of the window. "Desiree, wake up!".

Sharon coughed and dropped to her knees to scramble toward the bed. She reached out to the brass post at the foot of the bed and shook it as she called out, trying to waken Desiree.

Feeling her way along the side of the bed, she reached over Desiree's sleeping form and grabbed the blankets on the other side of the bed, yanking on them so that she could roll Desiree out of bed and onto the floor.

Finally the sheets and blankets came loose and Sharon pulled all the bedding, with Desiree unconscious between them and gently lowered the bundle to the floor. She was temporarily overcome with a choking fit, and buried her face in the blankets as she coughed, thinking "Oh God I don't want to die here."

With her face close to the floor, she gulped down a breath of air. Backing out of the room and pulling along the bundle of bedding with Desiree wrapped inside, she was thankful for the slippery smooth hardwood floor.

As soon as she had pulled the bedding past the bedroom door, Sharon lunged forward and slammed the door shut. The air was less smoky in the living room, and Sharon was able to run hunched over as she dragged her bundle, which was now emitting weak coughing sounds, through the kitchen and directly to the back door.

She pulled the door open and knelt down beside Desiree.

Desiree murmured "What is wrong. Where am I?", trying to sit up from her cocoon.

"We have to get out of here right away." She wrapped one of the blankets around Desi, who had closed her eyes again, and lifted her through the door, closing it on her way through.

Desiree started coughing again, and Sharon stepped over to the round patio table. "Desi, just sit up here for a minute." Pulling Desi to lean against her left shoulder, Sharon gently thumped Desi's back. Desiree raised her head. Her weak groan and partial cough frightened Sharon.

"Oh my God, Desi. I've got to get you out of here. Away from the fire." She felt a shiver through the blanket as Desi collapsed again into Sharon's arms.

Yanking the blanket tighter around Desi, Sharon lifted her up and stepped toward the edge of the patio. With her eyes watering from the smoke, she looked past Desi's car and down the roadway.

The only light was from the flames at the front of the house, and the faint glow from the highway through the trees. "Oh God. I hope we don't fall."

For her first few steps, the only thought in Sharon's mind was getting away from the fire and saving Desiree. She managed to find her way until she approached the fallen tree.

Setting her fragile parcel down in the smooth rut of the road, she whispered "Now Desi, don't worry. Just lay still while I pull you under the tree."

She climbed over to the other side of the tree and reached under to grab the edges of the blanket. Pulling slowly, hoping that Desi's shoulder wouldn't touch the rough bark above her, Sharon managed to slide Desi clear of the tree.

Lifting her up as she struggled to stand, Sharon whispered in alarm. "Oh God, my car keys, they're back in the house!"

Desi mumbled as she reached her arm up around Sharon. Sharon carried her to the side of the car and helped her sit up against the rear tire. "Now Desi, just sit here for a minute. I know you're just in your pajamas, but I'll be right back."

Running toward the house, Sharon could see that the flames had grown higher. "Oh no. There's going to be a forest fire if I don't call somebody."

She took one very deep breath and pulled up the front of her T-shirt to cover her mouth before opening the door. As the backdraft roared past her, she crouched down before running into the kitchen. "Thank heavens I left my purse on the floor" she thought as she grabbed her purse from beside the sofa, then turned to leave.

Hunched over as she walked past the kitchen table, she thought for a fleeting moment of all Desi's ornaments and treasures. She was wondering if she should try to save anything, when the kitchen door slammed shut in front of her. Jumping up in shock, Sharon could see the shadow of someone standing to the right of the kitchen door.

The realization hit her that this was no ordinary fire and danger was staring her in the face. She started screaming and made a frantic dash for the back door.

With her hand on the doorknob, she felt the sleeve of her T-shirt being grabbed. She yanked herself away and tried to swing her purse like a hammer toward the dark threat. Realizing how close the person was, she took a dive toward the form, her hands in tight fists, and shoved as hard as she could. Sharon hear a grunt as she felt the person fall against the wall behind.

In a split second she had grabbed the door handle again, pulled open the door and slammed it shut behind her. She flew over the patio toward the road, ignoring any concern for where her feet were landing, as she galloped through the bush to her car, afraid to look behind her, barely able to see the roadway in front of her.

Finally reaching her car, where Desiree had curled herself up on the ground, Sharon yanked her keys out of her bag and double-clicked the unlock button to open all the doors.

She lifted Desiree into the back seat and, fearing that the monster was immediately behind her, Sharon jumped into the car, slammed the door shut and pushed the "lock" button on her keys.

After she had curled Desi up on the seat, she lifted Desi's head enough to gently push her napping pillow into place. She pulled her afghan over Desi before crawling over the console into the driver's seat. Turning on the headlights as she started the car, she sighed. "At least now I can see where I'm going."

She maneuvered through the roadway, glancing with fearful eyes at her rear view mirrors after every bump, until she could see the main highway ahead of her. "Thank heavens we've made it" she muttered as she gave the car more gas.

Just seconds later, she slammed on the brakes when she saw a car at the end of the roadway, almost blocking her way up to the highway. "My god, whose car is that?" Her panic yelled back that it belonged to the person she had pushed in the house.

Gunning the engine, Sharon cranked the steering wheel, the tires of her car spinning as she fish-tailed her way up the incline onto the highway. She felt a bump at the back corner of her car, and realized that she had smashed the headlight of the lurking vehicle.

Moments later she was speeding down the highway, reminding herself of the mountain driving hints her late husband had given her.

She started muttering, "Slow down before the curves, then accelerate through them. Watch out for black ice. Watch out for deer on the road."

Thankful that the highway seemed to be virtually deserted, Sharon drove as fast as she could. Her mind racing, "I should phone 911 about the fire. Later. Not safe now." Glancing down to check the instrument panel, she whispered, "C'mon Betsy, don't let me down." She caught a flash of something in her rear view mirror.

Taking a closer look, her eyes wide with fear, she blurted, "Oh God. There's a car behind me. Missing a headlight!". Raw fear filled her mind.

"Where are the police? Don't they work at night in this Godforsaken country." Not daring to look again into her rear-view mirror, Sharon increased her speed on the next straightaway until her car was almost shuddering.

After what felt like hours of wild driving, Sharon sighed when the large "H" sign appeared ahead. She felt as though a guardian angel had just landed in front of her, and she slowed down to turn into the hospital emergency parking lot.

She raced into the emergency entrance and ran directly to the admitting clerk, calling out. "I need help. Please, my aunt's outside in my car. She's going to die." She turned around, ran back outside to her car, pulled Desiree out into the cool night air and scooped her up in her arms.

As she carried her aunt into the hospital, two attendants, rolling a stretcher between them, met her between the two sets of automatic doors. As they lifted Desiree out of Sharon's arms, she told them about the fire and how weak her aunt was.

Sharon watched as they wheeled Desiree through the swinging doors of the emergency triage, then sat down in a chair in front of the admitting clerk. She started to provide Desiree's information for admission to the hospital, when the relief of being in a safe place suddenly washed over her and she broke into tears, leaning her elbows on the counter.

"Are you all right miss? Here, let's find a place for you to rest for a few minutes."

As Sharon turned toward the sitting area, she glanced out the windows and saw a car pull into the parking lot. It's driver-side headlight was dark. Sharon felt nausea sweep over her. Everything went black.

"What happened?" Sharon asked a few minutes later, lifting her head from the floor. She rolled to her side and tried to sit up.

The nurse kneeling beside her grasped her elbow. "Don't try to get up just yet. I think you fainted."

Sharon rubbed her face. "I feel okay now. I'll just sit over there." As she stood up, the automatic doors opened and David burst into the waiting area.

"Sharon!" He ran toward her, his arms reaching out. "Oh, my angel. Thank heavens you're okay." He hugged her to his chest and rested his chin on the top of her head.

"Oh, David." She felt him shudder as he took a deep breath. Turning her face to look up at him, she muttered "You won't believe what's happened."

"I have an idea, believe me." He smiled at her as he took her hand and guided her toward the windows. "Let's sit down. I have some news for you."

"Desi's house caught fire. Somebody tried to grab me." The words tumbled out of Sharon's mouth, "I can still smell the smoke. And I forgot to call the fire department." Pausing to take a breath, she moaned, "Oh no, my poor Desi, she's lost everything."

David put his arm around her. "Okay, my dear, just calm down now. We'll get through this."

Sharon realized that this was the first time she had shown any vulnerability in front of David. Before now she had been priding herself on her independence and ability to cope with anything, but this time she just couldn't keep her guard up, and it didn't matter. She felt safe.

She turned a questioning look up at him. "You said you had some news?"

"After you left the office yesterday morning, I knew something was really wrong about your aunt's Will. Then I realized that those three other changed wills were all of former clients at Stewart & Company, just like your aunt, so I made some phone calls. Good old Fisher and his suspicious mind, he had already told the police, and they have been trying to track down the people named as beneficiaries in all of those wills."

"Why? To see if they are connected somehow?"

"I think that's the idea. But the really weird thing is that at least two of the beneficiaries seemed to be almost invisible."

"Now you're really losing me." Sharon shook her head.

"Well, the investigators went to the addresses of the beneficiaries and found that each person they were looking for had rented the apartment only a few months before the death of the testator who had named them in the will. In all cases, the beneficiary had since moved away without leaving a forwarding address."

Sharon sat up with a start. "We need to get them to check that person named in the Will Mr. Reese prepared. I think somebody's trying to kill Desi."

"I've already asked the police to check who that person is."

"Are they going to check Elizabeth Reynolds too? I met her last night when she came over for a visit. She and Desi seem like good friends."

"I think the police will focus on the person who was named as the first beneficiary. Mrs. Reynolds is only the back-up beneficiary in your aunt's fraudulent will."

Sharon sat for a moment, rubbing her chin with her finger. "I can't let Desi live alone any more." She looked at David. "Do you think your cousin will mind if she stays with me?"

"I'm sure that will be fine. Do you think they'll keep her long in the hospital?"

Sharon jumped up, "Oh, I forgot. I've got to give the admitting clerk the rest of Desi's information. They need to know who her doctor is."

David stood up and walked beside her toward the admitting desk. "By the way, I called 911 last night, and it was my car you hit."

Sharon stopped in her tracks, staring at David's grinning face. "What? You were up at Desi's at that time of night?"

"Yes. My last call with the police was around midnight, and by then I couldn't just leave you two alone up there." His grin turned into a chuckle. "By the way, you're quite the driver. I couldn't keep up with you, especially with only one headlight."

"David, I'm so sorry. I'll pay to fix your car."

"Never mind. Look, the clerk is here now. Let's sit down and get this over with. Then we'll go see how your aunt is doing before we get you home to bed."

The news of the fire and Sharon's heroic rescue spread quickly up the island, and by the next afternoon when Sharon woke up everyone was talking.

David had spent the remainder of the night on the sofa in Sharon's basement suite, leaving as soon as he knew his cousin's family was awake upstairs. He told them of the night's events and asked them to check on Sharon, but to not wake her before noon.

When David returned, he knocked on Sharon's door then opened it before she could get up from her kitchen table. "Hello there, my Amazon lady. How are you feeling?" He bent down to kiss her forehead.

His closeness felt familiar and comforting, Sharon smiled. "Other than my arms feeling like limp noodles. I feel fine."

"Would you like to visit your aunt?"

Walking into Desi's room at the hospital, Sharon was dismayed to see her hooked up to intravenous liquids and oxygen. "Desi." Sharon whispered as she touched Desi's hand.

Desi's eyes popped open as her hand jerked. She smiled and turned her hand to hold Sharon's, sighing "Oh, my. What a fuss I'm causing..."

Sharon could feel Desi's weakness. She bent down to kiss her forehead and murmured, "Don't try to talk, sweetheart. You need your rest for now. We just wanted to see you." Turning to David, she said "Let's go see if we can talk to the doctor."

Desi stirred and mumbled. "I'll be fine. I'm just sleepy."

Later, as they were leaving the hospital, David said "Do you feel up to talking to the police?"

Sharon looked at David in surprise. "Do they need to talk to me?"

"Yes. The fire department couldn't do much to save Desi's house last night, but they noticed the remains of a gas can at the front of the house, and a few other signs of arson, so they reported it."

Later that evening as Sharon and David sat in the quiet Italian restaurant finishing their dinner, Sharon sighed. "Thank you for everything, David. I feel much more relaxed now."

"You had a tough time at the police station today, didn't you?" He reached out to hold her hand.

Feeling that jump in her heart again, Sharon took a long breath. "It was like reliving the nightmare, having to give them all the details."

David chuckled, "And now they want your T-shirt too." He paused as he squeezed Sharon's hand. "Let's have a dessert coffee before I take you home."

"You're going to get me drunk with all this good stuff," she grinned.

"Not too drunk, I hope. I want to talk serious for a minute."

"Oh." Sharon pulled her hand away. "What's up?"

David sat forward against the table, looking directly into her eyes as he inhaled. "I don't want you to go back to Vancouver. You can finish your law degree in Victoria, and we'll find a place where you and your aunt can live together until we get our house built."

"Our house?" Sharon could feel tears growing in her eyes. "David, what are you saying?"

He reached across the table and held her hands. Grinning, he murmured "Three guesses." He stood up, still holding her hands and walked around the table. Bending down to put his knee on the floor in front of her, he looked up. "I don't have the ring yet, but will you marry me?"

Sharon dropped out of her chair, onto her knees in front of him and threw her arms around his shoulders, resting her head on his chest. "I will. I will."

Realizing that the waiter was staring at them, Sharon jumped back to her chair, laughing "Make a spectacle of myself."

David turned to her as he sat down in his chair. "Desi will like the idea, won't she?"

ABOUT THE AUTHOR

Lorraine Wait is a retired legal professional who started to write "The Other Face" many years ago while on a two-week holiday she had taken specifically to "get this plot down on paper." It was long before she had met her first computer or word-processer, and the paper was recycled and legal-sized, with one carbon copy. for revisions.

Raising her three children and launching her legal career kept her from indulging in more work on her story. It wasn't until she had switched to semi-retirement, about six years ago, that she took the time to transcribe the paper notes into a computer file, which grew into a 53,000 word story.

Lorraine has been writing for pleasure, as well as preservation of her spirit, since her teenage years, and treasures the memories and events she has recorded in over a dozen loose-leaf binders the size of this book.

Lorraine lives in southwestern British Columbia with her husband and their black and white Shi-Tzu, Sammy.

She hopes her readers will enjoy their visit to her make-believe world as much as she has enjoyed living through its creation.

"She was very rude to her mother, for one thing, and that really upset Donald." Desi smiled as she sighed. "Dear Donald, he was so concerned about good manners and kindness to family."

"Can you tell us anything else about your neighbors?"

"I remember one time Elizabeth was really upset because her daughter had quit her really high paying job in California. She had been working for the movies, doing wardrobe and make-up or something like that, to take secretary jobs in Vancouver. And she wouldn't talk about it to Elizabeth."

"Do you know if her daughter was ever married?"

"I think that might have been why her daughter left California. Elizabeth told me that her daughter had married a very wealthy older man in California. It was about a year after he died that her daughter came back to Canada."

"Do you know what her daughter's name was?"

"Betty is her first name. I'm not sure about her last name. It was 'Cameron' or 'Campbell' or something. Is that important?"

Sharon and David looked at each other, surprise flashing between them. Sharon turned toward her aunt. "We're not sure, Desi. The police will probably sort it all   out."

Several days after Sharon and Desi had settled themselves into their temporary home, David had dinner with them. As they all relaxed in the living room afterward, David brought up the subject of the will they had discovered in his office.

Desi was emphatic that she had not changed her Will. "It's still in my safety deposit box at the bank. I won't be making any changes."

Sharon had turned to David. "Desi has put me on as joint owner of all her assets. Her will is just a back-up plan if something happens to me."

David turned again toward Desi. "This other will we found, which we now know wasn't signed by you, named two beneficiaries, one of them being your neighbor, Elizabeth Reynolds. Have you ever thought of giving her a share of your property?"

Desi had straightened herself, indignation glaring from her eyes. "Absolutely not. That would never cross my mind, especially because my late husband didn't care much for her or her daughter."

"Oh. So they've been your neighbors for a long time?"

"Well, Elizabeth has been. After Donald met Elizabeth's daughter, though, he seemed to change his mind about my friendship with Elizabeth."

"So you were friends with Elizabeth?"

"We had lots of good talks over the years. She did have trouble understanding her daughter, though, especially when I talked about how wonderful Sharon has been to me."

"What was wrong with her daughter?"

CHAPTER 26

Two weeks later, Desiree waved good-bye to the nurses as she and Sharon walked arm-in-arm to the elevators. "We won't do too much shopping today. Just enough to give you a few outfits to wear for now."

"And then we'll go look at the apartment you've rented for us."

"Well, David is renting it for us. I'm sure you'll like it, though, with the view of the water."

Desi stopped. Sadness passed across her eyes as she looked up at Sharon. "My poor little house. I don't know who would want to burn it down."

Sharon didn't try to reply, knowing that no words of comfort would be good enough.

She and David had spent several hours with Desi while she was in the hospital, telling her about what they had discovered. As they left the hospital after one visit, Sharon had remarked, "David, I think Desi is having trouble letting herself think about things right now." They didn't pursue the subject after that.

Sharon rested her arms on the table, smiling. "She'll be delirious. She has been saying all along that you and I were 'meant for each other', in her words."

28298530R00155

Made in the USA
San Bernardino, CA
26 December 2015